PRAISE FOR USA TODAY AND WALL STREET JOURNAL BESTSELLING AUTHOR JAN MORAN

Seabreeze Inn and *Coral Cottage* series

"A wonderful story… Will make you feel like the sea breeze is streaming through your hair." – Laura Bradbury, Bestselling Author

"A novel that gives fans of romantic sagas a compelling voice to follow." – *Booklist*

"An entertaining beach read with multi-generational context and humor." – *InD'Tale* Magazine

"Wonderful characters and a sweet story." – Kellie Coates Gilbert, Bestselling Author

"A fun read that grabs you at the start." – Tina Sloan, Author and Award-Winning Actress

"Jan Moran is the queen of the epic romance." —Rebecca Forster, *USA Today* Bestselling Author

"The women are intelligent and strong. At the core is a strong, close-knit family." — Betty's Reviews

The Chocolatier

"A delicious novel, makes you long for chocolate." – *Ciao Tutti*

"Smoothly written…full of intrigue, love, secrets, and romance." – *Lekker Lezen*

BOOKS BY JAN MORAN

Sparkle

20th-Century Historical

Hepburn's Necklace

The Chocolatier

The Winemakers: A Novel of Wine and Secrets

The Perfumer: Scent of Triumph

Seabreeze Reunion

USA TODAY & WALL STREET JOURNAL BESTSELLING AUTHOR

JAN MORAN

SEABREEZE REUNION

SUMMER BEACH, BOOK 8

JAN MORAN

SUNNY PALMS

PRESS

Library of Congress Cataloging-in-Publication Data
Moran, Jan.
/ by Jan Moran

ISBN 978-1-64778-112-5 (epub ebook)
ISBN 978-1-64778-114-9 (hardcover)
ISBN 978-1-64778-113-2 (paperback)
ISBN 978-1-64778-116-3 (audiobook)
ISBN 978-1-64778-115-6 (large print)

Published by Sunny Palms Press. Cover design by Sleepy Fox Studios. Cover images copyright Deposit Photos.

Sunny Palms Press
9663 Santa Monica Blvd STE 1158
Beverly Hills, CA 90210 USA
www.sunnypalmspress.com
www.JanMoran.com

For my beloved family of readers.
And to those who value the meaning of family,
whether such kindred spirits
are related, chosen, or stumbled upon.

*T*he summer sun was setting as Ivy walked along the beach with her mother. Golden rays washed the sky with watercolor strokes of orange and purple. Ivy paused to slip off her sandals, enjoying the warmth of the sun-warmed sand and the cool rush of seawater.

"What was it you wanted to talk about?" Ivy asked, curious why her mother had asked to speak to her. *Alone*, she'd emphasized. Ivy caught a fold of her full cotton skirt in one hand, holding it as they strolled.

"It's about the reunion," Carlotta began. "You've done so much already. I didn't realize the inn would be so busy."

"We're full every summer now, so we expect that. And I want to do this for you and Dad. We all do." Her parents would leave after the event to resume their sail around the world. Although she loved seeing them pursue their dream, she would miss them. This was the least she could do for them.

"I appreciate this more than you know." Carlotta smiled and brushed her silver-threaded dark hair from her face, her turquoise bracelets tinkling against the sound of the surf. "Still, gathering the family has been an extra burden on you, especially coming so soon after the sorority reunion Shelly booked. You've been working awfully late on the new attic rooms."

Ivy still had more to do tonight before the new guests arrived. "We host a lot of events now, and Poppy has done most of the planning and coordinating for our reunion." Her niece was a whiz at scheduling and marketing. Ivy couldn't have managed the reunion or the inn without her. "And Shelly," she added, though her sister had been busy with her new baby the past few months.

"Poppy's a treasure, like all of you girls. And you must go easy on Shelly right now," Carlotta added softly. She gazed over the ocean. "Your father will love seeing everyone."

Detecting unusual hesitancy in her mother's voice, Ivy waited for her to continue, watching the gulls soar over the ocean waves beside her. This wasn't like her mother. Carlotta was usually direct and forthright.

Finally, Ivy asked, "What else can I do to help?"

Carlotta sighed and took her hand. "What I want most is for Maya to come. Would you help me reach her? I know you're busy, and I probably shouldn't impose on you, but as her niece, maybe you can appeal to her in a way that I can't."

Ivy sucked in a breath. "I didn't think you were speaking."

"No, but I reached out to her children."

"And?"

Carlotta shook her head.

Ivy hadn't planned on this new task, and there wasn't much time left. Maya was her mother's only remaining sibling, and it had been years since they'd seen each other. They'd had a falling out when they were younger, although her mother didn't like to speak of it. All Ivy knew was that the relationship had gone from strained to nonexistent.

Carlotta pressed a finger to the corner of her eyes. "It's been my fault as much as hers."

"Mom, I doubt that."

"No, that's the truth. I had opportunities I should have taken. I see that now."

Ivy bit her lip, wondering what she could possibly do. "I don't know how you think I can help."

"You're not a threat to her. At least, not like I am. And I've watched how you deal with tiresome guests at the inn." Carlotta smiled. "You've grown into this new role and become quite the diplomat."

Coming from her mother, that meant a lot to Ivy. "Aunt Maya is in a different class."

Carlotta slowed her step. "Families shouldn't splinter, *mija.* I've tried, but Maya won't take my calls."

"And you think she'll take mine?"

A strange look filled Carlotta's face. "I have a feeling she will. Ivy, I need your help in mending our relationship. I'd like you to get to know her and her children."

Ivy wasn't sure this was a good idea, or if it was even possible. Most of all, she didn't want to see her mother hurt. "Do you think she would be amenable to that?"

Carlotta stooped to pick up a shell. As she turned it over, she said, "I know this is a lot to ask of you."

Ivy pinched the bridge of her nose. Her mother seldom asked anything of her, and this had clearly been weighing on her. "What makes you think Aunt Maya might be receptive to speaking again?"

"We're not getting any younger. When I think of the time we've wasted…" Carlotta dipped her head.

Ivy noticed her mother's eyes were rimmed with red, and she put her arm around Carlotta's still-strong shoulders. Her mother was a force; she'd raised five children and ran an import business with her husband, and now she was helping Ivy's sister Shelly with her first child. Surely Ivy could do this much for her.

"I'll do what I can," Ivy said lightly, hoping she wouldn't regret it.

"No, *mija*. We must do more than that." Carlotta pressed a hand to her heart. "For weeks, I've had one of my feelings that I just can't shake. I have no idea why, but I feel it's imperative that Maya and I resolve our issues. Not only for us but for the entire family."

Ivy was at a loss for words. Her mother had a well-developed prescience, a sort of sixth sense about things that both impressed and unnerved Ivy. But she would never make a promise to her mother that she couldn't keep.

Carlotta gazed toward the horizon, which had deepened into a spectacular, jewel-toned show of the heavens. "Our family needs this healing, and I know you're the one to do it." She hesitated again. "I've had dreams about this, *mija*."

Ivy sighed with reluctance. "While I appreciate your confidence in me, if Aunt Maya won't speak to you, I'm not sure she'll take my call."

Carlotta gripped her hands. "You'll think of a way. I know you will." She paused. "I've seen it. And it's here...in this house."

Ivy blinked. "What is?"

"I don't know, but it's the answer to everything."

The fine hairs on Ivy's neck bristled. Her mother's dreams had foretold incidents on more than one occasion. Ivy had little choice but to believe her.

"Say you'll do it," Carlotta said with quiet insistence.

Ivy knew that look of determination. She'd inherited more than her mother's deep green eyes. Yet she had no idea how she could accomplish this enormous task. Maya had cut off Carlotta so completely, and her children, too.

Slowly, Ivy nodded. "I promise."

THE NEXT DAY as Ivy worked to ready guest rooms for a large party due to check in, her mother's words ran through her mind.

She'd already placed a call to her aunt's daughter, Diana, who lived in Chicago. All she could do was wait for a reply. Until then, she had plenty to do.

"I'm glad this is the last room." Ivy unfurled a white cotton coverlet over a guestroom bed. Through the open window, an ocean gust lifted the airy, summer-weight fabric, billowing it like a sail that could carry her around the world.

Her sister caught one side.

Shelly smoothed the cover. "I hardly ever made my bed in New York unless company was coming. I barely knew how. Now look at me." She laughed softly, glancing over her shoulder to check on her sleeping infant. "Making fancy sheet corners with a baby strapped to my back. A few days ago, I woke up and realized I've become our mom. Or worse, you."

"We should both be lucky to turn out like Mom." Ivy tried to ignore Shelly's dig, but it stuck in her mind like a splinter, bound to fester if left untended. As the youngest sibling in the family, her sister had always been the carefree wild child, and she loved to tease her brothers and sisters. Still, her mother's advice floated into her mind. *Go easy on your sister.* She smoothed the sheet and, with it, her tone. "You're not that party girl anymore, sweetie."

"Hey, I worked hard, too."

"Never said you didn't," Ivy said. She walked around the end of the bed, pausing to stroke little Daisy's silky, sunny hair. At just four months old, the sweet child was nestled into a snug cocoon. Shelly had wrapped a stretchy, daisy-print fabric around her shoulders and midsection and over her flowing sundress, fashioning a secure baby carrier.

How could it have been more than twenty years since her daughters were born? Was she making the difference she'd imagined she would at that age? Instead of giving in to that thought, she said, "Daisy has been so quiet and good-natured today."

"She's sleeping only because she was up half the night.

Thank goodness Mitch tended to her." Shelly sighed. "It's ironic that I used to be the one going to bed at daybreak, grabbing a couple of hours of sleep, then managing luncheon events."

Ivy detected a wistful note in Shelly's voice. "Do you miss it?"

"I miss the idea of it," Shelly said thoughtfully. "It was fun at first, but dealing with bridezillas and Olympic-level social climbers finally wore me out."

"So now you've imported them for a final summer hurrah." A friend of Shelly's from New York had reserved the entire inn for a sorority reunion, and the group would be arriving later.

Kneeling gently so as not to wake Daisy, Shelly tucked an edge of the sheet under the mattress. "I realize the irony, but Beth is cool. Driven, like a lot of New Yorkers, but she has a fun side."

The organizer, Beth Baldwin, was a television producer with a reputation for perfection. The Seabreeze Inn was far from that.

Ivy glanced around the room. They had made the rooms comfortable with fresh linens and antique furniture from the former owner. Still, the old beach house had its share of creaky floors and drippy faucets. "I hope they have a tolerance for shabby beach chic."

"They know it's not the Hamptons."

Ivy recalled what her mother said about dealing with guests. That often involved managing expectations and doing it with a cheerful attitude. People visited Summer Beach to unwind. Sometimes they just needed a little help to get them started.

Now that Ivy's children were grown, her mission in life had become caring for travelers. Summer was the season that guests often arrived to gather with friends and family, intent on creating magical memories of vacations, weddings, honeymoons, and anniversaries.

This summer would include a reunion of their own. And Ivy would do anything to fulfill her mother's wishes.

Catching a glimpse of the seagulls gliding over the beach outside the guestroom window, Ivy had mixed feelings about their family gathering. Although it would be a time for celebration and reconnection, it also meant her mother and father would return to their round-the-world voyage immediately afterward. Another year would probably pass before Ivy and her siblings would see them again. Most of all, Ivy worried that a disaster might befall their parents on their small sailboat on the open sea.

If this was the last time she and her siblings would see their parents, it was imperative that this family reunion would be everything Carlotta and Sterling could want.

But she couldn't think like that, even though those thoughts sloshed around the edges of her mind and spilled into cracks like tide pools. Instead, she had resolved to focus on the good times and memories they were creating. Still, that terrible thought lingered.

And now that had to include Aunt Maya.

Ivy pressed her lips together as she tucked another corner. These last couple of weeks, her emotions had zipped along a dizzying spectrum stretched tight and thin as thread, although she tried to hide her frazzled nerves. The pressure of dealing with a squabble of relatives she hardly knew was worry enough, but now, she truly had to rise to the occasion with her mother's request.

"Hey, you." Shelly punched a pillow, stirring Ivy's thoughts. "I've been thinking…these are just the kind of women who might be interested in our off-season specialty weeks. Our spa week was successful, so why not pitch them on another one while they're here? Or a gourmet cooking or wine week?"

"Sometimes even you amaze me," Ivy replied with a straight face.

Shelly lobbed a pillow at her.

"Hey," Ivy cried as she ducked. Still, her sister had gotten her attention.

"You deserved that."

The baby gurgled softly in her sleep. "And you're lucky you have Daisy on board. Come on, this is the last room. We're almost finished."

"Thank goodness. I can't believe I signed up for this physical labor."

Ivy laughed at that. Shelly had worked only half the day. Still, they were both eager to finish.

Ticking off her mental list, Ivy prayed the house wouldn't spring another leak or have an electrical blackout. It had to be on its best behavior now. Never mind an earthquake or fire... She shuddered slightly, banishing those memories. Since arriving in Summer Beach, they'd had their share of disasters, but they'd survived.

Shelly gave a wry grin. "I wish you could have heard the shock in Beth's voice when she called me to create the floral arrangements for an episode she was filming, and I told her where I'd gone. She thought moving here from New York was pretty gutsy of me."

"I can understand how your friends would think it was." Ivy picked up a pillow. Some of her friends in Boston had thought the same.

"For both of us." Shelly tossed a lace-trimmed pillowcase to Ivy. "You were the one who didn't have much choice."

"We always have choices," Ivy said, arching a brow. "Even if we don't like them or have to dig deep for alternatives. At that time, I planned to sell this place as fast as possible. Being an innkeeper wasn't what I'd ever thought of doing."

Shelly heaved a sigh. "Back then, I thought I was only escaping Ezzra and a going-nowhere relationship. Instead, I found my real life. Which I love," she added quickly. "I just wish it were easier sometimes."

"Welcome to motherhood—and running a business."

"No one told me how hard it would be." Shelly smoothed a hand over her shoulder, checking on little Daisy.

"We're lucky we landed here." Ivy plumped the pillows and arranged them against the carved headboard, admiring the beautifully grained wood she had polished to a sheen earlier. She was grateful to the original owner, who'd furnished the home with impeccable taste. Turning this old beach house into an inn had saved Ivy and Shelly and changed their lives.

For the better. Ivy straightened and rubbed her aching lower back. She felt how Shelly looked, even though her sister had arrived late and hadn't done half the work she had today. "Remind me to get more help next time we have to prep every guest room at once."

Shelly passed a hand across her forehead. "I have to rest, or I'll be a mess when they arrive. Want to join me on the beach?"

Ivy swung open the door. "Let's go." She needed a break as much as her sister did. Once again, she thought of her mother's advice and wondered if something else was behind it.

She followed Shelly into the vintage kitchen, the floorboards creaking beneath their steps. By the rear door, they kicked off their shoes and scooched their toes into the beach flip-flops that always landed in a jumble. Ivy grabbed sunscreen and sunglasses from a shelf, and the two strolled outside toward a pair of canvas-covered beach loungers with a burnt orange umbrella angled between them.

"This never gets old," Shelly said, easing Daisy from her back.

The summer sun was warm on Ivy's back, and she drank in the fresh ocean air. A colorful frisbee soared their way, and a dog leapt to snatch it before racing back toward a group of college-aged kids. With the last month of summer upon them, the beach was extra crowded. Bright umbrellas, coolers, towels, and beach chairs crowded the sand, and laughter rolled through the air as children raced from endless waves.

Ivy breathed in again, feeling the calming effect of the beach. Once summer arrived in Summer Beach, the scent of suntan oil was as ubiquitous as the steady sea breezes that cooled the effect of sunny rays. Focusing on the distant horizon, her mind reeled back.

Everything in life changes except the constancy of the wind and waves. This shimmering view had not changed since Amelia Erickson had built the grand old beach house a century ago. The former owner had christened the home Las Brisas del Mar.

And now, the home and this stretch of sand were Ivy's to steward through another century. Even unexpected blessings brought a new host of challenges, but that's what life was about, Ivy figured. Once you master one level of challenges, the universe decides you can handle more.

Bring it on, she thought. Family reunion and all.

She stretched on the chaise lounge, grateful to have a few minutes to rest. Their niece Poppy was at the front desk, checking out the last of the earlier guests and undoubtedly answering questions about what to do and where to eat in Summer Beach.

She and Shelly wouldn't be missed for a little while.

Ivy positioned her lounger in the sun and smoothed sunscreen over her face. They didn't have long—unless the large party checking in was detained, which often occurred with flights from the east coast. Better to be safe, she thought, squeezing another bit of lotion onto her fingers.

Overhead, palm trees swayed, their thick fronds rustling in the breeze and casting dancing shadows across the sand.

Beside her, Shelly cradled Daisy on her chest. Closing her eyes, her sister swept wayward strands of sun-bleached chestnut hair from her face. Shelly looked tired, even though Ivy and Poppy had cleaned and changed most of the guestrooms before she arrived for work.

Still, Ivy knew babies could derail even the best of plans.

Striving for levity, Ivy nudged Shelly and held out the sunscreen to her. "Remember when we used to lather on the suntan oil and bake ourselves in bikinis on the beach?"

"Maybe your generation." Shelly dotted sunscreen on Daisy's forehead before applying it to her own.

"Seven years is hardly a generation." Ivy lifted a shoulder and let it fall. "At best, you're only a third of a generation behind me. And I was watching you on the beach when we were kids. You had on just as much oil as I did."

"Only because you were the one putting it on me." Shelly sighed and pointed to her nose. "See these freckles? Yet another sign that I was abused as a child under your care."

"Freckles are natural."

"Then why don't you have them?"

"Genetics, I suppose. It must be something in the DNA. Mom doesn't have them, only Dad."

"Who has left us all for sunnier shores. He hasn't even seen Daisy yet. I hope he makes it back for the reunion." Shelly sighed as she stroked Daisy's fine golden hair.

"He will. If he doesn't, he'll have to deal with Mom." Ivy smiled as she watched her tiny niece. As exasperating as Shelly could be, Ivy's heart filled with love for her and Daisy.

The child blinked against the sunshine and lifted her head, though she was still a little wobbly, like those cute bobblehead toys. Daisy was awake.

The little girl's personality was emerging a little more every day. Her wide blue eyes took in everything around her, and she smiled and laughed easily now unless she was hungry or needed a diaper change. This was quite a change from the first sleepless months.

Ivy shifted her cotton floral skirt higher on her legs for

more sun. "Mom said Dad has been complaining about the winter weather in Australia, so this reunion is a perfect excuse for a mid-journey homecoming. Besides, I think they really miss each other."

Sterling and Carlotta Bay had arrived in Sydney after crossing the Pacific to visit their eldest daughter and her husband, who was from Australia. Her mother had told her that this was the longest period she and her husband had ever been separated.

"I think Mom misses everyone," Shelly said. "It must get lonely out there on the high seas. A year at sea—even with time in port—I can't imagine it. And they're not even halfway."

What a year it has been, Ivy thought as she listened to the familiar refrain of ocean waves. Just a year ago, she and Bennett had married in a whirlwind weekend—at almost the same time as Shelly and Mitch. Months later, with Daisy's debut, Shelly's life was forever changed.

The year had been a period of adjustment for all of them.

"I really miss Dad," Shelly said, drawing in her lower lip. "I wish they'd get this trip over with and come back."

Ivy lifted her face to the fresh breeze. "Mom says their sail is not a race but a journey—the voyage of a lifetime they'd long dreamed about. We have to understand that."

Beside her, Daisy gurgled with glee at a gull flapping its wings as it rose in flight. Ivy smiled at her delight. It had been years since they'd had a baby in the Bay family. She caught the child's soft fingers, surprised at her increasingly strong grip. "I wonder what Daisy will be when she grows up?"

"She loves birds in flight." Shelly nodded toward the gliding gulls. "Anything in the sky, actually. A helicopter transfixed her the other day. Maybe she'll be a pilot. Like Piper." Shelly shifted under the umbrella. "Speaking of Piper, have you seen the new community park lately? She's doing an incredible job of transforming the old airfield."

"It's really shaped up." The young pilot had executed an emergency landing on the abandoned airstrip months ago. An emergency medical technician had tended to her, and they'd been inseparable ever since. Now they were cleaning up the old airstrip with the help of Summer Beach locals.

"Sunny has been helping quite a lot." Ivy's heart tightened as she thought of her youngest daughter, who was in what seemed to be her perennial last year of college. Ivy suspected Sunny was stretching out the degree plan because she didn't know what she wanted to do in life.

At least Sunny was working at the inn and contributing, something her formerly spoiled child never would have dreamed of doing before her father died. Sunny still had her moments, but with her older sister living and working in Los Angeles in the entertainment industry, she seemed more motivated. Yet, so far, that motivation extended only to taking additional classes and delaying her graduation.

On the other hand, Sunny was exploring her options. Feeling conflicted, Ivy rubbed her neck as a twinge of guilt contracted her muscles.

As the sun cleared a cloud, Ivy tugged the brim of her straw hat lower, trying to relax against her jostling monkey-brain thoughts. They had just finished installing bathrooms in the attic rooms, converting those into additional, although smaller, guest rooms. She lifted herself onto an elbow and turned to Shelly.

"I'm not sure we should put guests in the attic rooms yet. Maybe we should encourage them to share the larger rooms."

"Not these women." Shelly expelled a breath. "I told you they didn't want to do that. You worry too much."

"With good reason."

Ivy had made sure Shelly warned Beth about the attic rooms, which weren't as spacious as others. She'd compensated with a fresh blue-and-white marine theme, down comforters, new linens, and fresh flowers. Beth was unfazed, but then, she had reserved the best room for herself.

Shelly huffed as she jostled Daisy. "We're lucky that Forrest could spare Reed to install the bathrooms up there. It's so bright with the new windows he and his crew installed. You did a great job painting, too."

"Sure could have used your help." Ivy tried to keep her tone light, but she sensed Shelly picked up on her resentment.

Their brother had given them the job at cost, and their nephew had managed the tradespeople, but Ivy figured she and Shelly could paint and save some money. As it was, the job had taken longer due to material availability, so she'd spent late nights finishing the painting because Shelly disappeared. In fact, she'd hardly slept last night finishing preparations.

No one else was available to help. Bennett had a city council committee meeting, and Sunny had a ticket to a concert with friends. Ivy had sent Poppy to bed so she could be up early to prepare breakfast for guests.

Shelly made a face. "Are you giving me the silent treatment now? If you must know, Daisy exhausted me. Besides, painting is your department. You're a lot better with paintbrushes."

"Only on a canvas," Ivy shot back. "Fine art is nothing like painting rooms."

Shelly only shrugged.

"We still have other parts of the attic to freshen up." When Shelly didn't reply, Ivy tried again. "You said you planned to cover the transformation on your video channel. So, you still can. Let's finish the job."

Shelly scrunched her nose. "The smell of paint bothers me now. I think my hormones went wacky with this whole pregnancy gig."

"Another excuse," Ivy muttered.

Shelly glanced away. "It's not. I've been——" She stopped short. "Oh, never mind. You wouldn't understand."

"Try me," Ivy said softly, casting another look toward her sister, but Shelly bent her head, fussing with Daisy's clothes. "You could tape off areas for me before I begin painting."

"Like a *sous chef* painter?" Shelly sighed as if Ivy were making a huge request of her. "Next time, I promise. But I have a lot of landscaping to catch up on." Gesturing to Daisy, she added, "This little one isn't making that job any easier."

"Whatever you need help with, let me know. I'll add it to my list. Between Poppy, Sunny, and me, we can help you manage."

"Gardening is what I enjoy, but... I can't seem to get back into the groove of my old life." Shelly glanced down at Daisy, whose eyes were fluttering shut in the warmth. She drew her fingers across the child's round cheeks. "We all have different skills, Ives."

"Let Sunny—"

"No, Sunny failed weeding. Remember how she pulled out my bulbs?"

Ivy looked pointedly at Shelly. "You told her to pull out everything that didn't look like a flower."

"Well, yeah, but there were bulbs attached to the bottom."

"Sunny thought the weeds had really big roots." Ivy laughed. "My daughter is a city girl. Unlike your horticulture program, they didn't teach bulb identification in her communications major. You have to be specific with her." She drew her lip in. "I'm afraid your dill is gone, too. But I'll replace it."

"Sunny is not to go near my tomatoes," Shelly said, jabbing the air with her finger. "She can trim herbs, but that's it. Seriously, no more weeding. I'll have a talk with her."

"You should make little garden signs that say basil, oregano, cilantro, and so on. Insert them beside the plants, just in case."

"I thought we were making less work for me, not more."

"They're your herbs."

"Which you all eat with gusto," Shelly said, stroking

Daisy's forehead until she yawned and closed her eyes again. "There she goes. The sound of the sea usually puts her to sleep."

Watching Daisy, Ivy nodded. "I'll show Sunny how to make tiny signs and show her where to put them. We'll have a crafts project, like when she was young." She touched her sister's hand. Being a new mother was not easy. Was she expecting too much of Shelly right now?

Yet, in the high summer season, Ivy worked hard to stay even in the business, let alone get ahead. The burden of the financial juggling was on her shoulders. She glanced at her sister. Even now, Shelly seemed distracted.

Ivy tried another approach. "Mom says Daisy is sleeping more at night now. That should help."

Shelly laughed softly. "I don't know if she's actually sleeping the entire night or not. Maybe she wakes up, but when her dead-to-the-world parents don't budge, she gives up and goes back to sleep."

"If she's not waking you several times a night, don't question that gift."

"I suppose not. Although the strange thing is, sometimes I still lay awake, listening for her cry or a change in her breathing. Then I'm totally sleep-deprived the next day. That sounds weird, I know."

"Not at all. You're a parent, now."

Shelly drew a breath as if to add something, but instead, she asked, "How's the treehouse going?"

"The floor is down, and the roof is up," Ivy replied, noting the tight strain in Shelly's voice. "Bennett and his friends have done a good job of it." Their apartment above the garage was already feeling less crowded with the extra deck off the rear. "But we don't have time to finish it until after the reunion.

Shelly lifted a corner of her mouth. "I noticed my husband wasn't involved with that."

Ivy had been relieved at that. "Mitch supplied coffee and

pastries. After the fiasco of trying to add Daisy's room onto your house, the guys have banned him from construction."

"He was talking about building a shed on the back of the lot," Shelly said, stifling a yawn. "At the rate he goes, that would keep him busy until Daisy starts school."

Ivy slid a look at her sister. "As long as it's not another bedroom on the house."

"No more babies," Shelly said, cradling Daisy. "One is plenty for us. For now, anyway." A weary smile curved her lips. "Maybe Forrest can lend a hand on your treehouse. Didn't you want to enclose it?"

"I'd like to screen it, but not for a while. The last thing guests want is to wake to the sound of hammering."

This was the busy season for Summer Beach, and the inn had been fully booked for most of the summer. Their mother was taking turns staying with their twin brothers, Forrest and Flint, and enjoying their families, while also looking after Daisy. Today, Carlotta had met friends for lunch, so Shelly had brought Daisy to work with her. Soon, after their parents returned to their sea voyage, that would be their new normal at the inn.

Just then, Poppy strode across the sand toward them. The summer breeze swirled her silky blond hair like a halo. "So, this is where you two are."

"It's only been ten minutes." Shelly raised a hand, shielding her eyes from the sun's glare. "Who's watching the front desk?"

"Everyone is finally gone. Besides, I can see the front door from here." Poppy shook sand from her sandals as she spoke. Glancing between them, she narrowed her eyes. "What's going on with you two?"

"Why does there have to be anything?" Shelly asked. "We're just a couple of moms relaxing on the beach, right?"

"That's right," Ivy said, trying to keep her mind off of Aunt Maya, too.

Poppy raised her brow in obvious doubt. "As Nana says, trouble follows you—especially in that old house," she added, nodding toward the inn. "If you discovered something—"

"For Pete's sake, don't jinx us," Shelly cried. "The last time you said that, silver dollars poured from the wall of a former maid's room. Two-hundred-sixteen of them, to be exact. Not quite enough for the car seat and stroller."

"Or to repair the plumbing and wall," Ivy added.

Poppy brightened. "But enough to bring in a lot more with those necklaces you're making out of them."

"There's that, I guess," Shelly said. "They sell as soon as I post them to my website. Beth reserved some as well."

Ivy asked, "Have we heard from her or any of her sorority sisters yet?"

"I gave her a courtesy call," Poppy replied. "Just to let her know we were ready for them and to see if there was anything they needed on arrival." Poppy grinned. "I reached her office first. I didn't realize she works for that reality show, the *Family Archives.*"

Shelly blinked up at her niece. After a moment, she said quietly, "Actually, Beth created the concept and produces the show. She's quite accomplished."

Poppy's eyes glimmered with excitement. "I've watched every episode. Imagine finding out you have long-lost kin. Not that we need more Bays in the family, but family history is so fascinating—even explosive. Some guests get into huge arguments over secrets others in the family didn't know about."

"It's not always like that," Shelly replied, sounding slightly defensive.

Poppy grinned. "It happens a lot. Those are the best episodes."

"People just like to know where they came from," Shelly said.

Raising her brow, Poppy added, "I bet a lot of them regret finding out."

Shelly picked at a thread on Daisy's shirt. "There are a lot of reasons people might want to explore their ancestry."

Turning the conversation back to the business at hand, Ivy asked, "Can you think of anything else we need to do?" While she still lived by her scribbled lists, Poppy had gone digital.

"I think we're ready for them." Poppy ticked off her fingers. "One guest is bringing her miniature poodle, so I've changed her room to one of the Sunset suites. Otherwise, we could have a problem with Pixie."

"That was smart," Ivy said. The Chihuahua belonged to a long-term resident.

Poppy perched on the edge of the sun lounger. "Several of the women are lactose and gluten intolerant, so I asked Mitch to make dairy and gluten-free cookies for the evening gathering. And the last text I received from Beth indicated they would arrive in about an hour."

"This is why Ivy and I can take fifteen more minutes to relax." Wincing, Shelly rotated her neck. "I've never made so many beds in one day. At least Daisy slept through it."

Ivy and Poppy exchanged a look. In truth, her niece had done more than Shelly today.

Poppy cast a glance over her shoulder. "Help me keep an eye on the front."

"Will do." Ivy was thankful for Poppy's thorough attention to detail. Her niece still had other clients for her marketing business in Los Angeles, but many were on extended holidays during the summer. "We can relax like this more after the reunions."

"I wish Dad would stay longer," Shelly said, blinking. "Those Zoom calls leave me feeling kind of empty. I didn't have time to miss our folks when I lived in New York. Now I'm back in California, and they take off."

Ivy touched her sister's shoulder. She felt the same, but she understood her parent's desire to have one last epic sail at their age. "Dad wants to take advantage of the good weather while they can. They'll be back."

"But look at all the time he's spent with Honey and Gabe."

"That almost sounds like jealousy," Ivy said lightly.

Shelly swept a finger under her eye and sighed. "I didn't mean it like that."

"I know you didn't."

Ivy could have pointed out that their eldest sister rarely got to spend time with their parents, but Shelly knew that. She only wanted her father to see Daisy. Ivy understood, but she also knew how difficult it must be for their parents to juggle time between children and grandchildren and pursue their passion for sailing while they were still active enough to do it.

Just then, a car pulled up in front of the inn, and Poppy frowned. "Those guests just left. They must have forgotten something. I'll be right back."

Ivy watched her niece hurry back toward the house. When Poppy was out of earshot, she turned to Shelly. "So, what was that about exploring your ancestry?"

"Nothing. Poppy was just making an assumption, and I didn't think it was right." Shelly lowered her eyes.

Ivy knew that look. Arching an eyebrow, she said, "What are you hiding, Shells? Spill it."

Shelly opened her mouth, feigning innocence. "It's not me. It's Mitch. And this is for Daisy." She touched her sleeping daughter's forehead.

Ivy waited.

"All right, stop looking at me like that. I planned to tell you. Mitch insisted we spit into tubes and send them to an ancestry service for DNA analysis. His parents didn't tell him much about their family history. I joined him in solidarity because he was nervous. We're doing this for Daisy's sake—to see if there's anything that runs in the family that we should be watching for."

"Like nosiness and gossip?"

Shelly tugged a lock of hair from her twisted updo and twirled it around her finger. "I'm serious, Ives."

"So am I."

"Whatever." Shelly flicked her hand. "Not that there are any surprises on our side, but it's Mitch's ancestors we're concerned about."

"I don't think you have much to worry about. Daisy is a healthy little girl. Even if she weren't—"

"Then I'd love her all the more," Shelly interjected. "If that was even possible." She stroked Daisy's back. "The tests measure the probability of different health conditions. We don't want to miss anything we could have managed better through an early diagnosis."

"I think you're doing just fine." A thought occurred to her, and she frowned. "Is Daisy ill?"

"No, nothing like that," Shelly said quickly. "I have friends who've done this. Just to be aware." She drew in her lower lip. "I don't want everyone to know just yet. Not until we get the results. Mom might worry, and I've been enough trouble on her visit."

"Hardly; you just had a baby," Ivy said. "I'd call this a joyful time." She could understand Shelly's concern, so maybe a DNA test wasn't a bad idea.

Shelly sighed. "I hope I'll remember it that way."

"You will." Ivy exhaled with a measure of relief. Daisy was such a precious baby—it would break her heart if anything happened to her. Still, some things were out of anyone's control.

With her first child, Ivy had been so worried about doing everything right. By the time her second daughter was born, she was far more relaxed.

While Ivy liked being informed, parenthood seemed more demanding today than when her girls were young. Information overload was a real concern, yet she couldn't fault Shelly for wanting to be the best mother she could be. She and Mitch were good parents, even if they were a little tense from time to time. They'd get used to the routine of child-rearing soon enough.

Even though Ivy was sure that Shelly's DNA order would yield no surprises, she wondered how they might handle such news in Mitch's family. He'd had enough difficulties in his life.

As Ivy thought about Poppy's comments, she gave a little shudder, imaging how she'd feel if someone in their family sprang a surprising story on them. Her mother certainly wouldn't. Nor would her father. Carlotta always said that Sterling was the most honest man she knew—even to a fault.

Don't fish for compliments from your father, Carlotta would say, chuckling at her admonition. *He'll tell you the brutal truth, but at least he'll say it with love.*

Ivy's skin prickled, and she rubbed the back of her neck. She glanced back at the old house. Just as Amelia Erickson had provided refuge in this home for secrets almost too great to bear, could their ancestors have harbored any of their own? She couldn't imagine that her mother or father would have concealed anything important from them.

Certainly nothing as explosive as what Poppy watched on that television show. Her family didn't have those sorts of relationships.

Except for Aunt Maya, Ivy quickly amended.

2

*F*ive more minutes, Ivy thought to herself, burrowing her toes deeper under the sand where it was cool and damp. Beside her, Shelly and Daisy were dozing.

Just then, a truck with *Woodson Construction* emblazoned on the side turned into the car court behind the main house.

Ivy frowned as she watched the truck ease to a stop. She touched Shelly's arm. "Axe just arrived. He's not on our schedule this week. Did you summon him?"

Shelly opened one eye. "This time, I'm not to blame. Wasn't that on your list?"

"Oh, my gosh, I must have forgotten," Ivy said, gathering her skirt. She'd spoken to her husband about calling Axe to tend to the new deck, but now she couldn't recall which of them said they'd do it. Her brother Forrest and his crew were very busy this year, and Axe had made repairs to Bennett's house on the ridgetop.

"No rest for you." Shelly closed her eyes again.

"Seems that way," Ivy muttered.

She brushed sand from her bare feet, slid them into her sandals, and strode across the beach toward the truck to greet Axe Woodson.

Axe stepped out, his cowboy boots thudding on the pavement and his large frame towering above her. "Good to see you, Mrs. Mayor," he said in a deep baritone voice. "Or do you prefer Madame First Lady?"

"It's still Ivy to you." She laughed at his use of what many people in town were calling her.

"Yes, ma'am." He touched the brim of his baseball cap as if it were a Stetson.

"Now you're really making me feel old." Wasn't it enough that her memory was slipping?

Axe chuckled. "It's just my Midwestern manners."

With his muscular physique, he was easy on the eyes, but he was also at least ten years younger than Ivy. She might be married now, but she could still appreciate an exceptional human form—in a strictly artistic sense, of course.

She cleared her throat. "Did we have an appointment? I'm afraid I must have forgotten it. We have a large party checking in soon." Frowning, she swept a hand across her forehead. High season at the inn was not for the unorganized. Yet, try as she might, unless she added a task to one of her lists, she was likely to forget it.

"Actually, your husband called me," Axe replied. "He said he'd meet me here."

Ivy breathed out in relief. Just then, Bennett pulled his SUV beside Axe's vehicle. He stepped out and kissed Ivy on the cheek.

Still, Ivy was surprised. She didn't remember Bennett saying he would meet Axe here today. "Did the ceiling fans for the deck come in?"

Bennett hesitated. "We wrapped up business at City Hall early today, so I thought I'd see if Axe had time for an installation. Turned out he did. Relax, sweetheart, I've got this," he added, smoothing a hand over her arm.

At his reassuring touch, Ivy nodded, gladly letting him take over. After a year of marriage, the unexpected sight of him still lifted her spirits. "I appreciate that. This afternoon will be so busy with the new guests arriving all at once." Beth had explained that they were meeting at the airport in San Diego and had arranged limousines to Summer Beach.

Bennett kneaded her shoulders and dropped another kiss on her cheek. "Do you need any help in there?"

"We've got this. But thanks." Ivy knew Bennett worked hard, too. She could take care of her business.

Bennett tucked a strand of hair behind her ear. "I'll see you after work then."

Turning to his friend, he motioned for Axe to follow him upstairs. Each man tucked a boxed ceiling fan under their arm before they hurried off.

Ivy watched her husband climb the stairway to the old chauffeur's apartment they were using now. She was still adapting to being married again; moreover, she was still shedding habits from her previous marriage. Unlike Jeremy, Bennett seemed to enjoy helping her look after the old house, making minor repairs when he could and calling on experts when needed.

As Ivy made her way into the kitchen, the door to the butler's pantry swung open, and her mother bustled through. She still wore her luncheon outfit of a gauzy floral sundress with strappy, low-heeled sandals and an armful of turquoise and coral bangles. Her hair was wound into a sleek chignon.

"You look nice," Ivy said. "How was lunch?"

"It was wonderful to see my old friends," Carlotta said, greeting her with a hug. "They're off to shop the afternoon away, but with your new crowd arriving, I thought I should return to help with Daisy. You three girls are going to be awfully busy."

"Shelly will appreciate that," Ivy said. "So do I." She paused, recalling the discussion. "Mom, about…"

"The reunion? Of course." Carlotta clasped her hands.

"I'm so grateful for what you're doing. We shouldn't lose touch with family." She slid onto a stool at the center island.

That wasn't what Ivy had in mind, but they needed to finalize those plans, too. She drew a tablet and pen from a drawer and joined her mother. "Let's make sure you've included everyone on the guest list."

Carlotta raised her brow in surprise. "The entire family, of course. Your aunts and uncles on both sides and your cousins."

"We need a headcount to make sure we're not overlooking anyone."

"All right, then." Touching her fingers, Carlotta reeled off names.

Ivy started her list. The immediate family, which included Ivy's twin brothers, Forest and Flint, and their families. "How about Honey and Gabe? Is there any way they can make it?"

"Your father says no. They're quite busy with their businesses. Elena will surely miss seeing her parents."

"So will I," Ivy said. She didn't get to see her eldest sister as often as she'd like.

Behind them, Shelly entered the kitchen with Daisy in her arms, flailing and crying, and Poppy beside her. Daisy had a set of lungs on her that Ivy had seen startle even the most stalwart, pious pelicans and send shorebirds skittering in fright. Shelly was trying her best.

"Anyone else to add to the guest list?" Ivy asked.

Poppy nodded. "Elena is driving down from Los Angeles with Misty. She has an assistant for the jewelry shop now."

Ivy remembered one or two distant cousins who hadn't been very friendly. Gently, she asked her mother, "Are there any you might not want to include?"

Carlotta shook her head. "My dear, family means everyone."

A wave of guilt washed over Ivy. Yet, one person could spoil the entire affair. In fact, it wouldn't be the first time. Ivy hesitated. "Have you had second thoughts about Aunt Maya?"

Carlotta pressed her lips together. "I'm quite serious."

Shelly's eyes widened. "I thought you two had a falling out."

"We're working on that." To Ivy, she added, "Have you called yet?"

"I left a message this morning."

"I heard her daughter is even worse." Shelly made a face. "I guess that side of the family falls in the category of keeping your friends close and your enemies closer."

"Isn't that what Machiavelli said?" Poppy asked.

"I believe it was Sun Tzu from *The Art of War*," Carlotta replied with a small smile.

"You're both wrong," Shelly said, raising her voice over Daisy and plopping onto a stool. "That line is from *The Godfather*." Daisy let out another shriek, and Shelly swung her in her arms. "Daisy is already frightened."

Carlotta smiled at these comments. "Maya has always been complicated, but she's my older sister, and it's time we put issues behind us." She rested a hand on Shelly's arm. "Would you like me to look after Daisy?"

With a look of relief, Shelly passed the fussy child to her mother. "She's been fed and had her diaper changed. I have no idea what's wrong."

"Maybe she's bored or misses the beach." Carlotta cooed to her granddaughter. "There, there now."

Carlotta bounced Daisy a few times and murmured to her. Shortly, the child stared up at Carlotta, transfixed by her dangly silver earrings and sparkling necklace. Daisy suddenly forgot about crying.

Shelly raised her palms. "I give up."

Her mother smiled as she rested the child against her shoulder. "It's common for children to torture their parents and be angels for others. Try not to take it personally."

While Ivy made the guest list, Shelly asked, "Do you think Aunt Maya still has that crush on Dad? Nana told me about that when I was little, and I've never forgotten it."

Ivy froze. She didn't remember that story. Was that what had happened between the sisters?

"Your father married me," Carlotta said, lifting her chin.

"Not that she didn't try," Shelly said. "She's been married a few times, too."

Her mother brushed off the comments, and Ivy admired her resolve. Carlotta and Sterling enjoyed a close relationship and a good marriage.

"Where are you getting your information?" Ivy asked her sister.

"I see her daughter's posts on social media," Shelly said. "Could Diana look more like Cruella de Vil if she tried?"

At the sink, Poppy spewed out a sip of water she'd just taken, and everyone laughed.

"There's nothing wrong with having a little gray hair," Carlotta replied with a look of reprimand.

"Dad has never mentioned them," Poppy said, blushing as she wiped her blouse.

Ivy realized the younger generation might not be aware of old family stories. Shelly was right about that black-and-white hairstyle though.

"Of the three sisters, Maya was always the drama queen." Carlotta sighed, rubbing Daisy's back. "If she and her family come to the reunion, I expect you all to welcome them."

Shelly darted looks at Ivy and Poppy. "We'll try."

As they spoke, Daisy watched the slow twirl of her grandmother's silver earrings, hypnotized by the motion. Her eyelids began to droop, and her little fists relaxed.

Shelly breathed out in guarded relief at Daisy. Leaning forward with an inquisitive look, she asked, "What really happened between you and Aunt Maya?"

Ivy slid a look at her mother. Conflict was etched on her face.

Carlotta replied carefully, "Maya often acted without thinking. She couldn't have known the outcome of her actions. We both miss Pilar and always will."

Poppy looked confused. "I'm not following."

"Pilar was our younger sister, who died when she was a teenager."

The kitchen grew quiet. It was more complicated than that, Ivy suspected, though she didn't know the details. Somehow, relationships had broken down.

Carlotta went on, "It's healthy to get rid of old feelings and grudges that no longer serve us." She gave them all a piercing look. "Family is family, after all. It's time you met them."

None of them had attended family events before. While Ivy respected her mother's wishes, she still didn't have a good feeling about this. Still, she dutifully added them to the list: Maya, Diana, and Robert.

Just then, a ring sounded from the front desk, and Ivy pushed away from the counter. "That must be our guests." At least they'd had a little rest.

Shelly rose and kissed the limp, rag-doll body of her sleeping child.

Nestling in the safe embrace of her grandmother, Daisy's only response was to sweep a pink fist to her mouth and squeeze her eyes tighter.

Like angels when they sleep, Ivy thought. And oblivious to all that was around them.

"Thanks for looking after her," Shelly whispered.

As Ivy left the kitchen with Shelly and Poppy, she considered how grateful she was for her sisters and brothers. Her mother deserved to have a pleasant reunion, so she tried to shake the feeling of dread that was creeping over what should be a happy event.

Making her way through the butler's pantry, Ivy nodded to herself. "Everything will be fine."

Shelly arched an eyebrow. "Are you trying to convince yourself or me?"

"All of us." Ivy tilted her chin. "We're adults, aren't we?"

"That never stopped anyone from acting stupid," Shelly said. "Or evil. If Aunt Maya and Diana come, maybe we should put them in Amelia's room and let our ghost have a go at them."

"If you believe in that sort of thing." Ivy sniffed her disapproval, though a shiver still coursed through her. "I prefer to think of our former owner as a benevolent presence."

Shelly's face brightened with a conspiratorial look. "Paige told me the renovation of her bookshop and apartment is almost complete, so the room should be available. I think only our best room will do for Aunt Maya. Maybe we could hold a séance and ask Amelia Erickson if she could perform a little number with rattling chains and slamming doors."

Ivy swatted Shelly on the shoulder. "No one is conjuring ghosts. Even if such things existed." If guests thought the inn was haunted, that would dry up business faster than a hot Santa Ana wind. "I thought motherhood would make you more mature."

Shelly laughed, although it sounded a little forced to Ivy.

"Where's the fun in that?" Shelly retorted. "If anything, motherhood just pushed me over the edge."

"Of the cliff of ridiculousness," Ivy said.

Shelly executed an eye roll worthy of a teenager. "You should learn to let loose, or you'll end up like Aunt Maya and Diana."

"I know how to do that," Ivy shot back. Granted, she might have been a little rigid when she'd moved here, but Summer Beach, with its laid-back vibe, had been working its magic on her. Wasn't that obvious? She'd never be as free-spirited as Shelly, but that wasn't a bad thing.

One of them had to be responsible.

Gesturing ahead, Poppy whispered, "Shush, you two. Let it go."

Her face flushing, Ivy realized that right now, that responsible person was their niece. After all these years, Shelly could still annoy her. She drew a steadying breath. Just ahead of them in the foyer was a group of thirty-something women in chic summer dresses. They were rolling their designer luggage inside. These guests didn't need quarreling sisters; they needed the rejuvenating experience that they'd paid to enjoy.

A statuesque brunette in a slim black dress led the way like a conquering general. She was clearly in charge.

Beth Baldwin, Ivy guessed. "Everyone look happy, or else," she hissed.

Shelly laughed. "Ditto, Ives."

Raising her eyebrows and spreading her arms, Shelly turned to the crowd of women in the foyer. "Welcome to the Seabreeze Inn," she called out.

3

"My darling Shelly," Beth cried, enveloping her in a hug. She turned to her friends. "This is the woman I've been telling you about. For years she designed the most extraordinary floral arrangements for parties and events at my home in the Hamptons. And for the set in New York." Acknowledging Ivy and Poppy, she added, "I produce the *Family Archives* show."

"I'm a huge fan," Poppy said. "I love all the family mysteries and DNA science you include."

"It's quite an undertaking, but the stories we find are incredible." Beth winked at Shelly. "And then we lost this one to Summer Beach. Of course, I had to find out why. Isn't that right?"

"Well, now you know," Shelly replied.

"And have you received your—" Beth pressed her fingers to her lips, cutting off her words.

"Not yet," Shelly said quickly.

How did Beth know, Ivy wondered.

"Let's get this party started with libations by the pool," Shelly said, changing the subject. "We're serving our classic

Sea Breeze cocktail and a new iced coffee we call Mocha Java Beach."

Ivy surmised that Shelly must have confided in Beth about her DNA order, although she couldn't understand why. Sometimes Ivy didn't know whether to strangle her sister or pity her.

Maybe her mother had felt that way about Maya.

While her sister went to the kitchen to prepare drinks, Ivy checked in guests, and Poppy assigned rooms. In talking with Beth, she learned the woman had been president of the sorority. "And where did you go to college?"

"A small private college outside of Atlanta," Beth replied. "After graduation, we scattered across the country. I had always dreamed of moving to New York and working in film and television. Even so, I was determined to stay in contact with my sorority sisters. So, here we are, ten years after graduation. Some of us are married with children, some also have careers, and a few are still looking for Mr. Right."

Another woman—the only one in blue jeans and a crisp white shirt—raised her left hand, wiggling her bare fingers. "And some of us have no interest in ever finding him. Again or otherwise." She turned to Ivy. "I'm Emma, by the way. I was always the rebel. Must be the red hair."

"You always prided yourself on being the unreasonable one," Beth said, lifting her nose. "Perhaps you've heard that my brother just married. But I'm still holding out hope for you."

"As long as you're not holding your breath," Emma shot back while the other women watched the exchange between the two in guarded silence. "I've changed since college."

"Woo-hoo, a rebel just like me," Shelly said, reappearing with a tray of icy glasses.

"I'm just joking," Beth cooed in a cool voice. She flashed a smile and cast a look of superiority toward Emma while a few other women lifted their glasses. "I've completely forgotten that you left my brother at the altar."

And there it is, Ivy thought. Every sort of reunion has its history.

"I wondered why you invited me now," Emma replied with an edge of sarcasm. She swept her arm across Beth's shoulder. "Remember when we were best friends?"

Beth blinked. "Why shouldn't we be again?"

"No reason. Other than we haven't talked since college."

Raising her eyebrows, Shelly cut in, "Better take a glass before they're gone."

While Emma and Beth helped themselves to the chilled mocha coffee and cranberry-and-grapefruit cocktails, Ivy shot a grateful look at Shelly. Still, she could tell others in the group were uneasy, too.

The women planned to meet by the pool, and Ivy and Poppy began to show them to their rooms. She hoped the animosity between Emma and Beth would dissipate so they could enjoy themselves, though some people seemed to enjoy arguing.

Not that it was any of her business, Ivy reminded herself. She had too much on her mind for that.

When she returned to the foyer, Shelly and Poppy were speaking in low voices at the guest reception desk.

"It's going to be interesting to see which one, if either of them, comes out the winner," Shelly said.

"This isn't a boxing match," Ivy said.

Shelly smirked. "I wouldn't be surprised if it ended up that way. Although I like Emma, my bet is on Beth. I've seen her in action—that woman always gets her way."

Poppy's eyes widened. "You should see her handle guests on the show who don't really want to meet lost relatives. She always ends up persuading them."

"Still, we don't speculate about guests like that," Ivy said. "And she is Shelly's friend."

"Not exactly. Beth was a client." Shelly crossed her arms. "She was demanding but never argued about the bill and always paid on time."

Ivy glared at Shelly. "We didn't need to know that either. Be careful; sound carries in this old house."

Poppy blushed and returned to work, though Shelly waggled her fingers and sauntered toward the kitchen.

Ivy wished she could talk some sense into her sister. Shelly hadn't really been herself lately. An edge of worry, exhaustion, or pessimism—maybe all of those—seemed to weigh on her.

Suddenly, she wondered if Shelly and Mitch were getting along. The stress of having and caring for a baby could strain a relationship—even the best ones.

Maybe that's why her mother had told her to go easy on Shelly. Instantly, Ivy felt a little guilty for arguing with her sister.

AFTER A FULL DAY, Ivy climbed the stairs to the quarters she shared with Bennett behind the main house.

As the sun sank in the sky over the Pacific Ocean, she paused, enjoying the endless view across the waves and the cool marine layer drifting across the hot sand. Visitors were folding up their beach chairs and umbrellas after a day in the sun.

"Not a bad commute," she mused, feeling gratitude and pride for what she and Shelly and Poppy had made of this rambling old home by the sea. She continued up the stairs.

While the old chauffeur's apartment provided her and Bennett with more space and privacy than the master bedroom she'd been in, it seemed to her that household math was way off. Two people seemed to need three times as much space to stay out of each other's way.

That afternoon when she'd called Bennett to see how the ceiling fan installation was going, he said that he and Axe had run into complications. *You don't want to be anywhere near here,* he'd told her.

She'd been busy with the new guests anyway. The sorority sisters had lingered by the pool reminiscing and catching up, so Ivy had served appetizers there instead of in the library as she usually did in the afternoons.

What a day, she thought, rubbing her neck as she neared the door. Beth had been sniping at Emma, who still held her own in the contest. Ivy expected they were in for a long weekend of that. As her family's reunion drew closer, she began to dread a similar situation.

Think fun, Poppy had said. Ivy smiled. She was probably right.

Ivy was glad when the ladies hurried away for an early dinner reservation at Beaches, a popular restaurant on Main Street.

She placed her hand on the doorknob of their apartment, but the door swung free before she could open it.

"Welcome home, my love," Bennett said, kissing her lightly on the lips. In one hand, he held a glass of wine aloft. "You're early. It sounded like the party was in full swing by the pool."

"They're off to an early dinner. Did you figure out the problem with the ceiling fans?"

Bennett chuckled and swept his hand across his chin. "We finally got them working."

"My hero." She threaded her arms around her husband's neck. He felt solid and inviting in her arms, with a faint whiff of lime and sandalwood from his shaving soap. His hair was still damp from a shower.

Smiling, he offered her the glass of wine. "Your first treat of the evening."

She sipped it, savoring the rich bouquet. "I think this is the Malbec I like so much." A guest from Argentina had sent a case of very fine wine to them in appreciation. They'd tucked it away for special celebrations.

Ivy stepped inside. Soft jazz was playing in the background. "What are we celebrating?"

"Besides your hard work today? I thought we'd christen our treehouse. Only I didn't think it was necessary to break a good bottle across the bow."

"That would be a terrible waste," Ivy agreed. "But we still have a lot of work to do on it."

"Is that so?" With his arm around her, Bennett swept her toward the new deck.

She felt a breeze from the open door to the covered platform Bennett had built off the back, bracing it from below. After the summer crowd left, they planned to finish it.

The music was coming from the deck. So were the flickering lights. Curious, she quickened her step.

"Oh, you've finished it," she said, pressing a hand to her heart, surprised at the additions he and Axe had made today. The deck was surrounded by palm trees that rustled in the light breeze, hence the name.

"Almost. It could still use your touch." Standing behind her, Bennett slid his hands around her waist and kissed her cheek. Overhead, a pair of fans with wooden blades carved like tropical leaves whirled lazily. A marine-blue, canvas-covered sofa grouping with cream and coral cushions sat on a woven sisal mat.

Ivy trailed her fingers along the cushions. "Isn't this the patio furniture I admired at Nailed It?"

Rocking on his feet, Bennett grinned. "When I was at the hardware store, Jen mentioned that you really like this set. George delivered it while you were checking in guests this afternoon. Your hand-painted pillows would look great on it, too."

Gratitude flooded her heart. Bennet had planned and

arranged all of this for her. "How did you sneak all this up here?"

Chuckling, Bennett replied, "It only took us about ten minutes to unload everything and whisk it upstairs. I hoped you wouldn't see us. Carlotta was acting as a lookout."

"But she was with Daisy in the kitchen…"

"With a perfect vantage point."

On a low rattan table in front of the sofa sat a pair of hurricane lamps, flickering with the light of sweet fragrant candles.

"Those smell heavenly." Ivy breathed in, amazed at what he'd accomplished. He'd even arranged a charcuterie platter on the table.

"The candles were Jen's idea," he added. "But I picked out the scents. Pikake blossoms from Hawaii."

She held a hand out to him. "Very romantic."

His face colored slightly. "I thought so, too."

A small rattan writing desk sat against the short wall that rimmed the deck. Bennett gestured to it. "That's where we can write or catch up on work. I found this at Antique Times. Arthur brought it over, and Axe ran electricity to the wall behind it."

Ivy noticed a glossy fiddle-leaf fig plant, a dracaena, and a pair of tropical palms. "And the plants? Don't tell me; Roy and Leilani brought them from the Hidden Garden."

Bennett grinned. "Just Roy."

"I had no idea there was so much activity going on right behind my back. Sounds like it was quite a party. Or an expertly engineered mission."

Bennett ran a hand over his closely cropped hair. "Axe arrived a little ahead of schedule. And we didn't count on you being on the beach at that time. I thought you'd be inside plumping pillows."

"Don't you dare minimize what I do." Ivy thumped his

chest. "I do a lot more than plump pillows around here. But I did that, too. Plenty of them, in fact."

Bennett pressed a hand against her cheek. "I didn't mean for it to sound that way. You're the most amazing woman I know."

Ivy smiled up at him. "Right back at you."

Warming to his touch, she turned into his hand and kissed him. They had an easy banter now that she loved. The setting sun cast rays across the deck, bathing the open-air room in rosy hues.

As she sank onto the sofa, tension drained from her body. "This is pure bliss. Thank you for such a wonderful surprise."

Bennett eased next to her, picked up another glass of wine, and touched it to hers. A clear ring filled the air. "To many magical evenings here." After touching his lips to hers, he added, "Let me know when you're hungry. I have garlic shrimp warming in the kitchen."

"From Mitch?" she teased, looping her arms around him.

He laughed. "I'll have you know that I diced the garlic and sautéed the shrimp all by myself. And I found some small, tender Italian artichokes I think you'll like. I broiled them, whipped up a remoulade, and prepared clarified butter."

"What a Renaissance man you've become," she said with a smile playing on her lips as he cradled her face in his hands.

Grinning, he said, "A guy picks up a thing or two in life. I once took a cooking class in Spain when I was on holiday."

"With Jackie?" she asked softly.

Bennett nodded. "Somewhere up there, I'm sure she's happy that you're enjoying the results."

"That's a sweet thought." The esteem that Bennett had for his late wife was another reason she loved him.

Drawn toward his magnetic hazel eyes, Ivy noticed the tiny crinkles at the edges and a faint outline of the sunglasses he wore on his morning runs. They had been working through initial adjustments to married life, and now she felt an ease growing between them. Even life's mundane activities, like sharing the housework, were more enjoyable with him.

Relaxing with her husband at the end of a day was an unexpected gift that life had served up to her—and at an age where she'd been feeling more frumpy than fabulous. Under his mesmerizing gaze, she felt young and desirable again—and very much in love.

She smiled up at him. In a world that promoted youth, to her, Bennett had improved over the years. The slightly shy teenager with a guitar she'd met on the beach more than two decades ago had morphed into a man who still took her breath away. Her summer crush had evolved into a love that grew richer with time, she thought, swirling her wine.

Not that they hadn't had their challenges, but the rewards were as sweet as the honeysuckle that scented the night air. And if the fates were willing, they still had much life stretching before them.

"I wonder what we'll be like at my parent's age," she mused.

"I like to think we'll be just as fabulous as they are."

"We should be so lucky," she said, touching her glass to his.

Bennett stared past her to the sea. A faraway look clouded his face, and he hesitated.

Ivy detected the shift. "What is it?"

"Let's do something this winter. Get out of here for a while. Take that honeymoon we've been talking about. Hawaii is still warm in winter."

Ivy's heart fell. "After Mom leaves, Shelly will need more help. I'm not sure I can commit to that in the fall. And then there are the holidays."

"How about springtime?"

Ivy glanced down. "That's when we start getting busy. The schedule is already filling up."

"You'll need a break sometime." Bennett tore off a piece

of a crusty baguette and placed a thin slice of Iberian ham and soft Camembert cheese on a plate for her. He placed the plate in front of her and then filled his own.

"I'll take a holiday soon. I promise." Ivy wanted to travel with him, but she needed to take care of the inn. At this point, she couldn't count on Shelly. "Are you ready to meet the rest of the family?"

"Sure. Hope I pass the reunion test."

"I can't imagine why you wouldn't." However, Ivy wished she could be as certain as she sounded.

Bennett curved up one side of his mouth. "Family dynamics can be complicated."

Realizing this truth, Ivy grew quiet. While Bennett was diplomatic, he wasn't one to back down on issues. As she pondered different scenarios, her stomach growled, and she remembered she had skipped lunch.

Shifting on the sofa, she asked, "Now, where's that second course I've been promised?"

"Coming right up." After stealing another kiss from her, Bennett made his way toward the kitchen.

Gazing around, Ivy imagined all the good times ahead for them in this tropical treehouse paradise. Breathing in the fresh salt air was invigorating. It was as if nothing could harm them here, safe in their cossetted perch overlooking the swelling sea and the distant horizon.

If only that could be, and for the rest of their lives.

We'll make it so, she decided, determined to maintain this life she'd fought so hard to create. Dividing her time between the inn and her husband and family required balance, and she didn't always get it right.

As she thought about the reunion, she glanced around the airy structure. Although Ivy wanted the event to be perfect, if personality clashes proved overwhelming, perhaps this would be their place of respite. Now, if only she could find a way to reach her aunt.

4

*W*hen Bennett strolled into Java Beach, Mitch gestured to him from the coffee shop's kitchen. The younger man had a secretive look on his face, and Bennett wondered what he was up to. He made his way toward his new brother-in-law past an old surfboard, vintage Polynesian travel posters, and clutches of people sipping coffee and enjoying the summer day. Business was brisk at Java Beach today.

Bennett was relieved to see Mitch in good spirits again. He could only imagine the stress he had dealt with in becoming a new father, especially given his upbringing with an abusive father. Yet, from what Bennett saw, that had built character in Mitch and given him the determination to overcome all he had endured.

Still, there were certainly healthier ways to build strong traits.

In comparison, Bennett's life had been relatively uneventful—except for losing his first wife, Jackie. But now, he was building a life with Ivy, and he was deeply grateful for this second chance.

He could hear Mitch talking to his assistant, who stepped

from the kitchen to take an order for a customer. Bennett poked his head inside.

"How's it going in here?"

"I've got something new for you to try."

His friend—whom he now considered his brother-in-law, even though he wasn't sure that was quite the right term—was plating a dish.

"Tell me what you think." Mitch speared a seafood cake of some sort with a fork and handed it to him.

"That's a keeper," Bennett said between bites. "Delicious. Is this crab or shrimp?"

"Both. I'm trying to differentiate my menu. Everyone on the beach serves burgers, but since my gourmet coffee creations have been a hit, I've been thinking about what I can do that's different. I'll still offer burgers. But I'll make them with different cheeses. Brie. Stilton. Havarti. I'll add sautéed mushrooms and caramelized onions."

"Options for the grown-ups." Bennett grinned. "Sounds delicious."

"Ginger's recipes are my most popular dishes, but I can't accept any more from her now that her granddaughter is making a go of the Coral Cafe." Mitch spread a sauce onto a small plate, added a bunch of arugula, and placed another seafood cake on top with care.

"Marina has sure raised the bar in Summer Beach." Bennett watched his friend's meticulous attention to detail. Mitch had come a long way since serving coffee in paper cups on the beach and sleeping in his car. He had been studying new techniques and trying to improve his craft.

Mitch placed the dish in front of Bennett with a flourish. "Marina serves good food. She's brought in serious foodies with her food festivals."

"Sounds like you have to keep up," Bennett said, issuing a mild challenge.

"Times change." Mitch ran a hand through his spiky hair,

bleached blond from the sun. "Poppy and Shelly are attracting travel and lifestyle bloggers to Summer Beach, what with the Seabreeze Inn and their new specialty weeks. They always mention the Coral Cafe's menu."

"Java Beach gets its share of mentions, too."

"For coffee and muffins. I'm trying to build the afternoon business with a limited menu."

"I thought you liked to close early to take out charter groups." Mitch had a side business that did well when the whales were migrating.

"I did, but you have no idea how expensive kids are. I figure I'll spend more on diapers than I did for my first surfboard."

"Daisy won't be wearing diapers forever." Bennett chuckled, though he'd spent plenty on his nephew over the years. But he enjoyed doing it. He sliced a piece of the shrimp-and-crab cake and swept it through the sauce.

Mitch shook his head. "Have you seen how much those tiny pieces of clothing cost? And then there's college. I want Daisy to go, even if I didn't."

"You just made a huge leap there," Bennett said, smiling. Cleary, Mitch had new-father worries. "Relax; you've got time."

"It doesn't seem that way. Starting over like I did, I'm behind in adulting. Being responsible for a kid is a big deal. I can't mess up." Mitch folded his arms and leaned on the prep counter.

"You won't."

"I need to make sure of it. I'll hire another cook for the afternoon crowd that's been gorging on hot dogs and chips at the beach. Bratwurst, I'm thinking. And some vegan options."

"Good idea." Bennett took another bite of the appetizer and gave his friend a thumbs-up. "That has to go on the menu."

"Next week," Mitch said, looking pleased with Bennett's

response. "Has Ivy been keeping you updated about this reunion?"

"She mentioned it." Bennett knew Ivy's immediate family, most of whom lived nearby, but he had yet to meet the extended family.

Mitch wiped down his stainless-steel workspace. "Shelly expects that as newcomers to the family, we'll be heavily scrutinized. And that's the last thing Shelly needs right now."

"I've got nothing to hide."

Mitch paused and smirked. "Yeah, speak for yourself, Mayor."

"Hey, I'm sorry. I didn't mean it like that."

Immediately, Bennett regretted his choice of words. Mitch had served a short prison sentence for theft several years ago when he was hardly more than a teenager. When he'd arrived in Summer Beach, he'd just been released. Later, Mitch had confided in Bennett, and he'd kept the younger man's secret as he built a new reputation and business in Summer Beach.

Mitch waved off his words. "This is the price I pay for my teenage stupidity. So, do I tell the relatives first and get it over with or wait until they find out and confront me?"

"Mundane as it sounds, honesty is the best policy, but you probably shouldn't lead with that."

"Suppose not." Mitch shook his head. "I'll just wait until it comes up in conversation. Or maybe I'll find a weekend charter for the duration of the reunion to save Shelly the embarrassment."

Bennett touched his friend's shoulder. "I'm sure it won't be like that. No one will bring up your past."

Mitch hung his head. "No one but Google. It's easy to find out about me."

"Who cares? You and Shelly are married, so that makes you part of the family. And you're pretty successful now." Bennett gestured toward the cafe. "Can't argue with this."

Mitch gave a sarcastic chuckle. "You're too optimistic. I know how people are."

"Everyone in Summer Beach has accepted you. Even Chief Clark."

"Sure. Once my name was cleared, he released me from jail. With my record, I'll always be suspect number one."

"It won't be like that again." Yet even as Bennett reassured him, he knew that Mitch was being realistic.

No one had known about Mitch's past when he arrived in Summer Beach. But when his prior troubles came to light, there had been talk. The extended family might have a similar reaction. Yet once people got to know Mitch, they usually liked him.

"Good thing you don't have anything in your past to hide." Mitch raised an eyebrow. "I hope family members don't bring any expensive jewelry to lose on the beach."

Bennett nodded in thought. He hadn't checked himself out online—not that he had anything to worry about. There were a few cases against Summer Beach that he'd been involved with, the most notable being the lawsuit that Ivy's former husband had filed against the city. Jeremy had attempted to change the zoning to build his high-rise monstrosity. Still, Bennett wasn't concerned. Unlike Mitch, he'd lived life carefully.

Too carefully, though?

Bennett wondered. He didn't even have a bucket list. Marrying Ivy was the most adventurous thing he'd done in years. He'd seen plenty of men his age make drastic changes. His father-in-law was sailing around the world. His former neighbors, Tyler and Celia, had reconciled, and they were planning a long voyage, too. Roy and Leilani closed Hidden Garden every winter for a long holiday in Hawaii.

What was he doing with his life? Balancing the city budget, listening to the same minor complaints, and showing real estate on the weekends. The most exciting thing he was doing right now was building the extension on the chauffeur's cottage.

And he couldn't even talk Ivy into taking a holiday with him.

Was life passing him by?

"Hey, man. Earth to Mayor; come in, please." Mitch rapped his knuckles on the counter. "Did you hear anything I said?"

"What? Oh, sure."

"So, the answer is yes?"

"Absolutely." Bennett pushed aside his empty plate.

Mitch grinned. "Okay, then. This should be fun."

Bennett had no idea what Mitch had said, but whatever it was couldn't be earth-shattering.

Nothing in his life was.

Which is just the way he'd planned it. Still, he had a sense that he was missing something.

"There's one more thing I need your opinion on," Mitch said, looking concerned. "It's about Shelly. Ever since Daisy was born, she'd been kind of different. Tired, but more than that, and I'm not sure..." His voice trailed off as he glanced at a customer who'd just arrived at the counter.

Bennett heard the sudden shift in his friend's voice, and it worried him. He wondered how Mitch was adjusting to fatherhood. Due to the abuse he'd suffered as a child, he'd had some trepidation before the baby was born. He'd had counseling, but something was clearly on his mind. "Want to talk about it?"

Mitch ran a hand through his spiky hair. "That would be cool. It will have to be later."

"I won't forget." Bennett gave Mitch a hug and left Java Beach, strolling down Main Street toward the marina.

As Bennett walked, he thought about everything he had to be thankful for. Yet, sometimes he felt he was living in the shadow of the Seabreeze Inn in Ivy's heart. At that thought, he slowed, not knowing whether to chuckle or chastise himself. How could he be envious of an old house? He hoped he was more evolved than that.

Besides, he was the mayor of Summer Beach. He had achieved every goal he'd set for himself. Last year, he declined an important position that would have taken him from the community. He had no regrets about that.

Bennett glanced back at the inn, rising against the clear blue sky. Still, the vague feeling of discontent persisted. A thought formed in his mind, and he nodded to himself.

A man needs to matter to those he loves the most.

5

*S*itting in the library, Ivy clutched her phone and waited. She'd gotten this number for Aunt Maya's daughter after doing some sleuthing online. A woman answered. "Is this Diana?"

"Who wants to know?" came the haughty reply.

"This is Ivy. I'm your cousin." Quickly, Ivy spilled out everything she could about the reunion. "We'd love for you and your brother to come. And my mom would love to see your mother."

A pause ensued, and Ivy wondered if Diana was still there. Finally, she said, "Did you talk to my mother about this?"

"I left a message for her."

"Robert said your mother had called. My brother talks to her more than I do. I have no idea if they're going or not."

"Could you find out and let me know? Or let me know what it would take? My mother really wants to reconnect. Maybe they'd both like that before too much more time passes."

"You mean, before they die."

Ivy almost gagged. Diana was certainly direct. "It's my mother's greatest wish."

"Good luck with that. My mom's greatest wish is to have pasta in Italy before she dies. Her favorite place in the world."

Ivy tried again. "We'll reserve our best ocean-view rooms for you. We're right on the beach."

"Well, this is frightfully short notice, but I had a cancellation."

Suddenly, a thought occurred to her. "Do you have your mother's mailing address?"

Diana rattled off the address before hanging up.

Ivy drummed her fingers on the desk, thinking. *Italy, huh?* Clearly, her done wasn't done. She turned to her computer and looked up a famous Italian grocer that shipped delicacies. After browsing, Ivy clicked on the deluxe basket assortment. *A pasta assortment of gnocchi, orecchiette, and cavatelli, plus tiramisu, a bottle of wine, and Italian chocolates.*

It sounded delicious, and it might just work.

After tapping the number on her phone, she placed an order for delivery to her Aunt Maya's home in Chicago. "And could you include a gift card?"

"What do you want it to say?"

"Until we meet for dinner in Italy, would you join us at our family reunion in Summer Beach? All is forgiven, you are missed, and I would love to see you again. With love, Carlotta."

Ivy hung up and crossed her fingers. It was worth a try.

WITH THEIR SAND shoes and sunglasses, Ivy held the kitchen door open for her mother. They were picking up party decorations in town for the reunion, but her mother liked to take the beach route there.

As they left the house, she thought about the DNA test Shelly had told her about. Although her sister had asked her to keep this confidential, Ivy had a nagging feeling that she should inform her mother before the results arrived.

Maybe Shelly's DNA test would hold long-buried secrets. Or none at all, which was more likely. In which case, it wouldn't matter. But if something were revealed, Ivy would want her mother to be prepared.

As they walked along the surf, Ivy turned to her mother. "Do you think a DNA test might reveal any surprises in our history?"

"Why do you ask, *mija?*"

"We're all old enough to understand any family secrets. Look at the web of secrets and concealments that Amelia left."

"Finding the old paintings and crown jewels before Jeremy could demolish the house was a gift from the universe," her mother said.

"I haven't thought about it that way." By now, Ivy was beginning to accept that Amelia's spirit might have something to do with their finds—not that she was ready to admit that to Shelly, of course.

Carlotta squeezed Ivy's hand. "I doubt if we have any surprises in our ancestry. If you were looking for sizzling stories in our family, I'm afraid I must disappoint you—unless you want to reel back to the days of the Spaniards and how our ancestors received the Spanish land grant here in California. Unfortunately, only the barest of our family details remain of that period."

"Didn't someone contact you about that right before you left on your voyage?"

Carlotta shrugged. "Occasionally, a historical scholar finds a shred of new information, but it doesn't change who we are."

"You're sure about that?" Ivy hesitated. "Because Shelly sent off a vial of saliva for DNA analysis. I thought you should know before you and Dad left again. Just in case there was anything you might wish to tell us."

Drawing back, Carlotta looked surprised. "What motivated Shelly? We know who our family is."

"That's what I told her. But there's a lot that Mitch doesn't know about his background, and they're keen to gain any medical insights that might be helpful to Daisy."

Carlotta raised her eyebrows. "Sometimes I think it's better not to worry about what might lie ahead. Most of what we worry about never comes to pass." She fixed a piercing look on Ivy. "Like your concerns about our journey."

Ivy gave her a sheepish grin. Her mother knew how worried she was about their trip.

"Have we sunk the boat yet, *mija?*" Carlotta pursed her lips.

"You still have the other half of the world to sail around, Mom. Don't jinx things."

"We're quite capable of managing this voyage." Carlotta laughed and swung her arms over her head, lacing her fingers and blinking in the bright sunshine. "Besides, a good challenge keeps the heart pumping. Especially at our ages."

Maybe seventy is the new fifty, Ivy thought. Her mother's hammered silver bangles jingled on her slim, tanned forearms, which looked taut and muscular. Sailing could be hard physical work. Despite their age, her parents had clearly risen to the challenge.

"I know you're experienced, and I trust your judgment," Ivy said. That was what her mother needed to hear. Still, her trepidation persisted.

"We must embrace life," Carlotta said, drawing a deep breath of salt air. "Making plans is fine, but why worry about anything other than this moment? The past is history, and the future is unwritten. We create our lives as we go along."

"That's what I'm talking about," Ivy said. "I wouldn't want Shelly to have an unpleasant surprise because someone made up part of our history—and I don't mean that you did.

I'm also thinking about the reunion. I don't want anything to spoil it."

"And nothing will. Save your worry, sweetheart." A look of nostalgia illuminated Carlotta's eyes. "I want to make your Aunt Maya part of our lives again. She's not as bad as you think."

Ivy wasn't sure. "Do you really think that's possible?"

"I'd rather be an optimist and occasionally wrong than doubt possibility and always be right."

She had a point, Ivy allowed.

"So, have you spoken to her yet?"

"No, but I spoke to Diana this morning. I told her we have ocean-view rooms waiting. And I sent a basket of Italian food to Aunt Maya." She told her what she'd included on the note. "I hope you don't mind, but I figured I should try something different."

A faraway look filled Carlotta's eyes. "Dinner in Italy? I'm sure we could arrange that. Oh, I do hope she comes."

As they discussed plans for the reunion, they walked on, watching shorebirds plucking at the sand, seeking treasures and treats in swirling eddies like beachcombers sweeping the dunes. With the news Ivy had given her, Carlotta had brightened. She seemed so much happier just at the prospect.

Ivy thought about her parents and where they would stay. She had given her friend Paige her old room after the earthquake had left the older woman's bookshop and the apartment above it uninhabitable. They'd created space for a temporary bookshop on the lower level of the inn.

"Bennett, Mitch, and Captain Clark are helping Paige move out soon," Ivy said. "Axe and his crew have completely restored her shop and her quarters above it." Ivy would miss seeing the bookseller every day, but Pages Bookshop was a short walk from the inn.

"I hate to see Paige go," Carlotta said. "It's been so handy having a bookshop at the inn."

"Guests love it, too, but Paige is thrilled to be moving home. I'll miss her. Just like Imani and Jamir."

"Have you seen Imani's new house?" Carlotta asked. "Her floral assortment at Blossoms is so creative. I imagine her home is just as lovely."

"She asked me to visit, so I'll stop by soon," Ivy said. "After Paige leaves, you and Dad should take my old room."

Carlotta shook her head. "We can stay with Forrest or Flint. Give that room to Maya."

"But you two should have privacy and room to relax. You haven't seen each other since Daisy was born. As for Aunt Maya, we can elevate another room especially for her. Imani's room was quite large."

Carlotta appeared to consider this. "We can take that one. I believe I still have a credit card on file with the proprietor."

"Mom, you and Dad don't have to pay—"

"Nonsense," Carlotta cut in. "We keep it in the family."

"Seriously, I won't let you."

"Then I'll find something else to do for you." Carlotta linked arms with Ivy and rubbed her forearm. "Your father and I have worked so hard to create our good fortune. Let us spoil our grown babies a little before we go."

"By *go*, I hope you mean sailing." Ivy shuddered. She couldn't imagine a life without her parents, even though they were often thousands of miles away.

"None of us know how long we have, so we must live each day as if it might be our last."

"Mom, please don't talk like that. You sound like Dad now."

"That's the *unvarnished truth*, as he would say." Carlotta laughed. "Although we're in excellent health and still feel youthful, we must also be realistic. You do know about our last wishes. Now that Daisy is part of the family—"

"Mom, we'll all take care of Daisy, and you're not going anywhere."

"We all have a time. That's what makes living so much sweeter. The older you become, the more you'll realize that." Carlotta smiled. "As for traveling, that has been part of our lives for so many years. After your father's visit, we plan to sail for South Africa."

As much as Ivy would miss her parents, she realized that someday they might not have the energy or health to do as they pleased. This was a sunny window for them—after children and before the vicissitudes of health might inhibit their independence.

Once her parents returned from their round-the-world voyage and moved back into their home, which they'd rented out for the duration of their trip, Ivy vowed to spend more time with them. With that in mind, Ivy smiled at her mother, thankful that her parents were living the life they wanted.

A thought struck her. Someday, she would walk this beach with only the memory of her mother for company. But that was not today. Grateful for Carlotta's presence, she grasped her hand and marveled at the energy and life force that tingled in her mother's firm grip.

Carlotta peered at her as if reading her thoughts, the light in her eyes reassuring Ivy. "And what a grand time we'll have in South Africa," Carlotta continued. "Did I tell you about our old friends we're meeting in Cape Town? They have a thriving vineyard and a beautiful wine cave where they host receptions and weddings."

"Tell me again, Mom," Ivy said, clutching her mother's arm and enjoying her enthusiasm for life.

As Carlotta talked about their friends, Ivy wondered if someday she would grow to be more like her mother, with her ability to seize and enjoy moments without overthinking them.

Her mother had always loved throwing parties. For as long as she could remember, her childhood home had been the center of activity, with every birthday, holiday, and party celebrated there. "Consider my home yours now," she added.

"Your home is your livelihood, too." Carlotta lifted her face toward the sun. "It's been too long since we gathered your cousins. If only Maya would return my calls."

"She sounds like a prima donna."

Carlotta laughed. "My sister has had a spectacular life, but she always had a big heart. Most of the cousins will be happy staying with family." She paused. "Your father would insist that we give Maya the best room."

Ivy shook her head. "You're not paying for her room at the inn."

Carlotta paused. "It's Tia Maya, remember? You'll wish you'd charged more. And if by some miracle, Honey and Gabe make it, you'll have to put Honey at the opposite end of the inn from Maya."

"Wasn't that disagreement years ago?"

"Maya never forgets an imagined slight."

"What exactly happened?"

Carlotta sighed. "Honey was younger and prettier than Maya, so she was certain that her husband at the time had an eye for her."

Ivy hadn't heard this part of the story. "Did he?"

"He had elegant manners, but no. He was besotted with Maya, though heaven knows why. I believe that was the last time I saw her."

Ivy shook her head, amazed at the stories still coming out.

"And then there's your cousin Elberto, the history professor who wouldn't hurt a gnat. Maya used to prey on Bertie like a tiger, intent on shredding his dignity."

"Clearly at opposite ends of the sensitivity spectrum," Ivy said. "We'll be sure to separate them."

"Oh dear, I forgot," Carlotta said. "Bertie won't be able to make it."

Ivy pursed her lips. "Maybe we should put Aunt Maya in the attic and be done with her."

Laughing, Carlotta hugged Ivy. "Good for you. I would expect that from Shelly, but you were always my kind child."

Ivy shook her head. "Who is also tired of being taken advantage of."

"Well then, Jeremy must have served a purpose after all. Not to speak ill of the dead, that is," she added softly, touching her hand.

"It's nothing I haven't thought, Mom. I wanted a good marriage so desperately, but now, comparing him to Bennett, I realize that I brainwashed myself into believing it. After the initial whirlwind romance waned, I couldn't admit—even to myself—that my life was less than perfect."

Her mother squeezed her shoulder. "I'm sorry to say it now, but the signs were there, *mija*. You must pass that learning on to your daughters."

"If they'll listen," Ivy said. "I remember you'd often ask me about our relationship, but I thought if I ignored the signs, they'd go away. All I wanted was a normal family life for the girls."

"You managed that for quite a while. Even though, in retrospect, it was a tenuous—and ultimately untenable —situation."

"I understand that now." Ivy recalled the weeks at a time Jeremy would spend out of town, saying that his client insisted he stay for the weekends for golf or working dinners. As their relationship deteriorated, she'd kept a brave face and chose to dismiss the signs. When his mistress fought Ivy for the inn after his death, she realized she'd been deluding herself.

She drew a breath, reminding herself that she'd already made peace with those remembrances and cast them out to sea.

Nudging her mother, she said, "I'm through with difficult people. If Aunt Maya misbehaves, I'll talk to her. Respectfully, of course."

"Bravo," her mother said, laughing. "I'll do the same."

Ivy smiled. "Honestly, how much trouble could she be now? Surely she's mellowed."

"Maya and I have a lot to talk about," Carlotta said quietly. "Things we should say before we…"

Ivy put her arm around her mother. "You'd better not say *die* or *get lost at sea*."

Laughing, Carlotta shook her head. "The former is inevitable, *mija*, though not for a long time, I hope. But promise me you won't take all the responsibility for the reunion upon yourself."

"I won't," Ivy replied. "Poppy is a dream. She's super organized."

"And a lot like you in that regard." Gazing toward the waves, Carlotta shifted the conversation. "I've been thinking about Shelly, too."

A knot formed in the pit of Ivy's stomach. She was still irritated over Shelly's recent behavior. "She's been awfully busy with little Daisy."

Shelly managed to care for the garden, but she had grown less dependable since the baby was born. It had been a long time since Ivy's children were young, but she'd always managed. Why couldn't Shelly?

"I've noticed you two have been bickering more than usual."

"She's always been slightly—what's the word? Irreverent, I guess. But now that often crosses the line into sarcasm. Sometimes I'd rather do things myself."

"Shelly needs help right now. That's why I've stayed so long, even though your father and I miss each other."

"Children are not a perennial excuse."

Her mother smiled. "She's always had a sharp sense of humor and follows her heart." Carlotta paused. "So, when I noticed a change in her, I suggested she see a doctor."

Ivy considered this. "I remember being so tired and overwhelmed after Misty was born, but not as much with Sunny. I suppose it's only natural to feel that way."

Ahead of them on the beach was a group of teenagers playing volleyball. Carlotta gestured toward a wide flat rock that jutted toward the sea. "Let's sit before we go on."

Ivy followed her, and they eased onto the sun-warmed stone.

Carlotta drew up her knees and clasped them. "Most of my pregnancies and deliveries were fairly easy, and I always managed to juggle the children. Except for one time."

Ivy didn't recall this, and she was interested. "Go on."

"Coincidentally, it was after Shelly was born. You'd think by the time my fifth child came along, it would be easy." Carlotta shook her head. "I could hardly get out of bed, and I snapped at everyone. I just didn't have the will to do much. It was as if all my energy had been sapped, and I was sad for no reason."

"I never knew that." Ivy would have been seven years old at the time. She tried to recall that time, but her memory was fuzzy. Still, what her mother said sounded familiar.

Watching her, Carlotta said, "You were very young, and back then, we didn't talk about things like postpartum depression."

Ivy's lips parted with surprise. "Are you sure that's what it was?"

"We used to call those first couple of weeks after giving birth the baby blues. That is, when you feel overwhelmed, a little sad, and sleep deprived. But my symptoms went on for much longer."

A connection floated into Ivy's mind. "I felt a little like that after Misty was born."

"You were fortunate," Carlotta said. "I've been at the beach cottage with Shelly more than you have. I've been observing her, so I suggested she seek help. She is now going to group meetings with other mothers. That's why she was late this morning. She dragged herself out of bed to go."

"Why didn't she tell me?"

"You can be intimidating, Ivy. She sees you as the perfect older sister who has her life together."

Ivy was aghast at that thought. "*Perfect* isn't even in my neighborhood, let alone the house I live in. But then, that's how I thought of Honey." From the outside, her older sister's life in Sydney seemed as perfect as a postcard. Now, she knew it hadn't always been that way.

Carlotta touched her shoulder and nodded. "Sisters can be complicated. Shelly will tell you when she's ready."

"Now I feel guilty for thinking she was lazy." Ivy pressed a hand to her forehead. How could she have missed the signs? "I should have noticed."

"You did; you saw a change in her behavior. Shelly is so spirited and energetic that her low speed is average for most people." Carlotta's expression softened. "You've been adjusting to a new marriage, plus you've been busy with the summer crowds. Shelly started treatment a few weeks ago. It might be too early to tell, but I believe she's improving."

"Thanks for trusting me with this. Since you've been gone, I often feel like I'm mothering—or maybe smothering —Shelly."

Carlotta raised her face to the sun. "She's always been our starry-eyed child full of wonder and delight. Each one of you came equipped with your unique personality. You were the patient, long-suffering artist. Though you've discovered a fresh appreciation for life here."

Ivy considered that. "I'm not sure I like that description of me, although it probably fits." Since she'd arrived in Summer Beach, she had certainly grown, yet she often felt she still had a long way to go to gain her mother's sense of adventure and freedom. "And Honey?"

"She inherited our love of travel and thirst for new experiences," Carlotta replied. "We weren't surprised when she moved to Australia with Gabe."

Ivy was enjoying these insights. "What about Forrest and Flint? I always found it interesting that Forrest loved carpentry and construction while Flint was fascinated with ocean life. The land and the sea—they couldn't have had more different passions."

"While each has his interests, the twins are two halves of the same coin." Carlotta raised her brow and smiled. "Both are responsible, hard-working family men—like your father. And your husband."

"If he'd had children, that is."

Carlotta eased from the rock and shook sand from her sandals. "That time has passed, and Bennett has embraced your family. Your father is so at ease with him that he calls him his third son."

Ivy joined her, and they turned toward the village. "And Mitch?"

"Another wild child like Shelly," Carlotta replied, grinning. "They share a spark of creativity and love of freedom—of living outside the bounds." With a hint of mischief, she arched an eyebrow. "I can't imagine where they get that from."

Ivy smiled; she knew Carlotta was often Shelly's source of inspiration, and Ivy saw so many similarities between them. "I hope Shelly will develop your wisdom someday."

Carlotta chuckled. "Oh, you got an extra helping of that gene. But there's hope for her, too. I was more like Shelly before I married. Wisdom comes with age. If you're paying attention, that is."

"I hope so," Ivy said. "We'll have a lot of different personalities at this reunion."

Nodding in agreement, Carlotta said, "It's good to know your people, even if you don't see them often. Now, about the reunion schedule…"

Ivy and her mother approached the village, discussing

details about the event. Yet, as they spoke, she had a gnawing sense that this reunion would have a profound change on their family, although she couldn't imagine why it might—or why she felt that way. Maybe it had been the conversation about their Aunt Maya, but surely they could handle an eccentric older woman. More concerning to Ivy now was Shelly's health.

Priorities, Ivy told herself as she listened to her mother outline her vision for the long reunion weekend. That's how she would manage.

As a gusty sea breeze whipped in from the sea, Ivy clasped her hair in one hand and opened the door to the shop that sold party decorations. If she could oversee a full house of sun-seeking vacationers, surely she could entertain a few high-spirited or opinionated relatives—and look after her sister.

6

*A*s Ivy languished on their new open-air balcony with Bennett, the palm fronds swished in the ocean breeze. Raucous laughter and off-key singing punctuated the balmy evening air. Those were the usual sounds from happy summer crowds. Living at the inn, Ivy had grown accustomed to that, though tonight's party was louder than most.

The sorority sisters had been there several days. "It's going to be awfully quiet when they leave," Ivy said.

Bennett grinned as he scooped their dessert from the electric ice cream maker, the latest addition to their treehouse. "Sounds like they're having a good time by the pool."

"They've spent the day at the beach and had dinner in town," Ivy said. "They'll probably wind down soon."

The group had taken over most of the inn, so Ivy wasn't concerned about them bothering others. Their long-term guest, Gilda, usually wrote at night with headphones.

Bennett handed her a bowl. "This chocolate chunk recipe is excellent. Next time, let's try it with pistachios, too."

Ivy took a bite. "Mmm, it is good. You spoil me."

"It's my pleasure." Bennett dropped a kiss on her forehead.

"I'll take an extra-long walk in the morning." She was glad Bennett loved her just the way she was. She might not have a bikini body anymore, but she felt good for her age. And she got to enjoy dessert.

But no more starving herself to please her former in-laws. Jeremy's mother still fit into the tiny Christian Dior suits she'd bought for her honeymoon decades ago, and she'd expected the same from Ivy. While Ivy had admired her mother-in-law's dedication to near starvation, after having two children, she couldn't be bothered to maintain a handspan waist anymore. There were more important things in her life.

Like cheesecake and tiramisu.

Outside, the singing grew louder, and a loud splash sounded. Ivy grinned between bites. "I think we're in for a long night."

She had grown accustomed to that, as had Poppy. They usually rose early to prepare breakfast. Sunny was out with friends tonight, and she probably wouldn't be back until later. Paige had confided to her that she could sleep through almost anything once she removed the discreet hearing aid she wore.

"It doesn't happen often. And they're having a great time." Bennett returned with a small bowl of ice cream and sat beside her, stretching his long legs on the coffee table.

"That ice cream maker was the best idea ever," she said, savoring every bite of the rich, creamy treat with dark chocolate chunks. "I remember when my brothers and sisters used to take turns with a crank on an old wooden tub filled with rock salt and ice."

Bennett chuckled. "My sister and I did the same. It was old-school, but that was half the fun."

"Maybe with those muscles," she said, playfully squeezing his arm. "I was sore for days. It was worth it, though. There's nothing like ice cream at the beach on a hot summer day."

"I should mention that to Mitch," Bennett said thoughtfully. "Maybe he could add home-churned ice cream to the menu."

"If he made an amazing coffee ice cream, he'd have a line out the door. Any flavor, actually."

As they were talking, a scream suddenly split the night.

Ivy jumped, startled. Immediately, her old lifeguard training kicked in. "I have to see what happened. Someone might need help."

Bennett swallowed his last bite. "I'll get my first aid kit."

As a volunteer firefighter, Bennett was also trained as a first responder. They headed for the door. She flung open the front door and tore down the stairs, her bare feet slapping on the wooden steps. As she did, she looked out over the pool to see what was happening.

Her jaw dropped. A stranger—a woman not much older than she was—wearing a leopard-print jacket, a turban, and reams of gold necklaces stood by the pool looking aghast as the sorority sisters pulled Beth from the water.

Ivy gasped. Fortunately, she looked conscious and was moving, but that wasn't why Ivy hesitated.

Damp swimsuits were flung around the pool. The women had been skinny dipping.

"Hold up," Ivy said, pressing a hand against Bennett's chest. "I'm not sure you should go down there."

"If someone is hurt..." His voice trailed off. "Oh. Well, I see what you mean."

Ivy passed a hand over her forehead. Surreal or absurd, or just women letting loose, she couldn't decide which it was. Not that it bothered her, but she wasn't sure about Bennett.

And who was that woman in the turban? She was definitely out of place.

"I'll take care of this," Ivy said.

"This isn't the first time I've seen an unclothed woman."

"But all of them at once?"

"They can get towels. Beth might need help."

He was right. "Let's go." She hurried down the stairs. "Coming through," she called out as she approached the throng of women.

"Excuse me," the strange visitor said, looking perturbed.

"I'll be with you in a minute." Ivy pressed her lips together. Whoever had the nerve to interrupt her right now could just wait.

The women parted, and as they saw Bennett, a couple of them screamed while others dove for towels. A few seemed oblivious. Lining the pool were champagne bottles and glasses, which explained a lot.

Pushing dripping strands from her face, Emma knelt beside Beth and frowned. "She hit her head on the edge of the pool." She gestured toward the strange visitor. "That woman surprised Beth, and she stumbled at the edge and fell. She slipped under the surface before I could reach her."

"Well," the other woman huffed. "It wasn't my fault. The front door is locked. Whoever is supposed to be tending the front desk should be fired."

Ivy held up a hand to the woman. This was the last thing she needed right now.

"Beth almost drowned," another woman exclaimed. "Emma saved her life."

"Let's have a look at you," Ivy said to Beth. She smoothed a hand over the woman's scalp and felt a lump forming, but there was no laceration. "How are you feeling?"

Beth pressed a hand against her forehead. "I feel a monster of a headache coming on," she said, slightly slurring her words.

Ivy chewed her lip. Alcohol and a head injury—not a good combination.

Behind her, Bennett draped a towel over Beth's bare shoulders and handed one to Emma, who suddenly realized he was there.

"Oh, thanks," Emma said, a little embarrassed. "We were just having some fun. Is she going to be okay?"

"Most likely." Bennett opened his bag. "Has she been drinking?"

Nodding, Emma gestured toward the empty bottles. "But Beth started earlier than most of us."

Concerned for their guest, Ivy held up her index finger. "Follow my finger," she said as she moved it from side to side.

"Slow down," Beth said, wavering a little.

At least she was communicating, Ivy thought as Bennett took her blood pressure. But Beth's gaze was unfocused, whether, from alcohol or injury, Ivy couldn't tell, but they couldn't take a chance. She leaned in toward her. "You hit your head quite hard, so you should be checked out more thoroughly. We can call an ambulance to take you to our local hospital."

"On it," Poppy said behind them. "I wasn't really sleeping anyway." She was wearing a cotton robe hastily tied around her waist. As she pressed the phone to her ear with one hand, she handed out towels from a stack on a chaise lounge with the other.

The new woman threw up her hands. "Am I invisible? I'm here to check in, and instead, I have to vie for attention with this bacchanalian revelry."

"Ma'am—" Ivy began. This evening was going sideways fast, and she didn't need whoever this person was hovering over her.

"A low-class group of hussies," the woman finished, glaring at the others around her.

"Wowzer," one of the sorority sisters called out. "I don't think I've ever been called a hussy. We've still got it, girls! Who wants more champagne?"

Bennett drew a hand over his mouth, and Ivy could see he was trying to keep a straight face as he knelt beside Beth.

Fortunately, Beth was laughing, too.

Ivy glanced back at Poppy, grateful for her niece's help. With Bennett tending to Beth, she looked up at the older woman. With her chic outfit and layers of jewelry, she resembled Coco Chanel in her later years. But she looked completely out of place in Summer Beach.

Ivy didn't have time to deal with this woman. "I'm sorry, but the inn is full tonight. Did you reserve a room?" She hoped they hadn't taken a reservation by mistake.

The woman drew herself up and gave Ivy an imperious glare. "I shouldn't need one."

Again with the attitude, Ivy thought. Striving to remain cordial, she said, "The Seal Cove Inn might have a room. We can call a taxi for you if you don't have transportation."

The woman's mouth dropped open in shock.

Ivy ignored her. Thankfully, they didn't get many guests like that. Ms. Fancy Entitlement would have to wait while they tended to Beth.

"I don't want to go anywhere," Beth said, clutching her head. "Tell your niece to hang up the phone."

"That's not a good idea," Ivy said patiently. "You could have a serious brain injury. You're a smart woman, and you wouldn't want to ignore that."

Emma leaned in. "If I wake up and find you dead in your bed tomorrow morning, I swear I'll never forgive you. Neither will that sassy mother of yours—or any of us."

Beth pulled the towel tighter around her shoulders. "Okay, I'll go," she said grudgingly.

Ivy nodded at Poppy, who spoke quickly into the phone.

"I'll wait," the entitled woman announced. She flounced to a chair and plopped down. "And would someone turn down that annoying music?"

Bennett jerked his head in Ms. Entitlement's direction. "Want me to deal with that woman?"

"I need you to stay here with Beth." Ivy scanned their

guest's face, afraid that she might have really injured herself. She needed Bennett here with her, not off tending to some high-maintenance woman they didn't have room for anyway. Ms. Entitlement could wait.

With any luck, she'd leave.

Ivy continued talking to Beth to keep her engaged. Within a few minutes, an ambulance arrived, and a pair of emergency medical technicians hurried toward them.

"Hi, Noah," Ivy said, recognizing the young man who'd looked after Piper, another one of their guests, a few months ago.

Noah greeted her and Bennett. "What's going on here?"

Bennett filled him in while Ivy helped Beth with a towel. Noah and his partner examined her injury before helping her into the ambulance.

Beth turned around. "Where's Emma? I need her."

"I'm coming," Emma said, looking determined.

Beth reached for her friend's hand. "I'm so, so sorry for anything I might have said to you. I haven't been acting very nice, have I?"

"Forget it," Emma said. "We're sisters, remember?"

Beth hooked her little finger with Emma's and smiled. "Forever. And you know what? My brother wasn't good enough for you."

Off to one side, Ms. Entitlement gave a loud huff. "Imagine. Grown women, acting like children." She pulled out her phone.

Ivy hoped she was calling the Summer Beach taxi service.

Noah's partner tended to Beth, and he walked around the vehicle to talk to Bennett and Ivy. "Good to see you both. Come see the park when you can. Piper is doing an amazing job."

"You bet," Bennett said, shaking his hand. "And take good care of your passengers here."

"Always," Noah said before climbing into the driver's seat.

As the ambulance turned into the night, the women around the pool began to disperse, picking up their clothes on their way.

Ivy, Bennett, and Poppy were left by the pool.

"That was quite a party," Ivy said. "I wouldn't have expected that from the prim and proper ones."

"They're the ones you have to look out for," Poppy said.

Crossing her arms, Ivy said, "No, that would be Ms. Entitlement over there. I should deal with her. As soon as she gets off the phone, that is." The woman was gesturing in anger, and whoever was on the other end of the line was getting an earful. Ivy felt sorry for whoever she was talking to.

Bennett brought a garbage bin to the patio. "I'll take care of the rest of this."

"Thanks," Ivy said. "I don't think they'll be up very early for breakfast. Poppy, you can sleep in."

Ivy stifled a yawn. "Yet another night to remember. Shelly will be sorry she missed this."

Bennett chuckled. "I can just imagine her reaction."

As Ivy picked up a forgotten swimsuit top and draped it over a chair arm for its owner to find later, she laughed along with him. "Never a dull moment at the Seabreeze Inn."

She only hoped that Beth was okay. They'd never lost a guest, and she didn't want to start now.

When Ms. Entitlement put her phone down, Ivy strode across the patio toward her.

"Thank you for your patience," Ivy said. "Now, I can call the Seal Cove Inn for you to see if they have a room for you."

The woman stood abruptly. "That won't be necessary. I called my aunt, whose daughter owns this establishment, and I told her about this travesty. She's calling her daughter right now. And I'll wager that you, miss, are about to be fired." She gave Ivy a dismissive wave. "You should pack your things."

Through the open door of their apartment upstairs, Ivy

heard her phone ring. Her heart sank, and she blinked at the woman. "Are you my cousin Diana?"

"And you are?"

"We spoke on the phone a few days ago. I'm Ivy." And we're off to a blazing start, she thought.

7

*I*vy felt the weight of Diana's glare. Instinctively, she pressed her back against the kitchen countertop, but she had to deal with this new arrival. If this was the daughter, Ivy dreaded meeting the mother. Next to her, Bennett clutched her hand while Poppy lingered near the door as if ready to flee.

Diana drew herself up like a medieval ruler. "Must we tarry in the kitchen like servants? First, my flight was delayed for hours, and now this."

"Easy," Bennett whispered, squeezing Ivy's hand. "Did you find a room for your cousin at the Seal Cove Inn?"

"It's sold out." Ivy had woken the proprietor at the other inn in town. But after the long last weekend of summer, the town would empty out. That's why they had planned the reunion for next week.

"Well, you can certainly make room for me here. Simply move someone." Diana flicked her hand as if disposing of a troublesome insect.

"It's too late for that." Ivy was horrified at Diana's nonchalant attitude toward kicking a guest from their bed. "But we will find a place for you. And I've called my mom."

Poppy intervened. "Let's go to the parlor." Holding the kitchen door for Diana, she mustered the courage to speak to their formidable relation. "I'm Poppy, another cousin. Would you care for a cup of tea or a glass of wine while we figure this out?"

Ivy gave Poppy a wan smile of encouragement.

"Tea? At this time of night?" Diana shot Poppy a withering look. "And I only drink wine with meals. However, you may offer me a digestif."

"A what?" Poppy asked.

Diana arched a finely drawn eyebrow. "A liqueur or cordial would be appropriate." She raised her eyes to the ceiling. "Have you all been raised like wolves?"

Ivy couldn't resist. "More like coyotes. It's Southern California."

Poppy's smile froze on her face. "Okay. How about brandy?"

Ivy wasn't sure if Poppy was asking her or Diana. Beside her, Bennett coughed. She could tell he was trying not to laugh, so she edged an elbow into his ribs.

Diana gave a derisive sniff. "Cognac is my preference."

Poppy's eyes widened. "Almost the same thing, right?"

"I suppose I must spell it out," Diana replied, pressing her fingers to her temples. "Only Cognac is from France, dear child."

Turning to her stricken niece, Ivy struggled to maintain some semblance of cordiality. "I'll see our cousin to the front parlor." With a subtle lift of her chin, she added, "Would you bring her a glass of our finest French Cognac? It's in the butler's pantry."

Thankfully, Poppy recovered, nodding as if she were a practiced connoisseur. They still had the brandy they'd used to make iced Brandy Alexanders for a pool party not long ago. *Ice cream, brandy, and crème de cacao with a dash of nutmeg.* All they could do was pass off brandy to Diana as French Cognac, though Ivy had her doubts. Still, a nightcap after the evening's chaos and her cousin's long trip was definitely in order.

As Ivy led Diana toward the parlor, she heard her mother call out from the front door.

"Diana, dear," Carlotta cried, rushing toward her niece. With her face devoid of makeup and her hair in a braid, she wore a cotton robe over her pajamas. "What in the world are you doing here? The reunion isn't until next week."

"No, you're wrong," Diana said. "You clearly stated that it would begin tomorrow. Has Mother arrived?"

Carlotta laughed and hugged her niece. "I think I know the dates of the reunion I'm hosting. But I can understand the mix-up. And I'm glad you arrived early. That will give us much more time together. I hope your mother can join us."

Ivy was certain of the dates she'd given Diana. Nevertheless, her mother gave an award-winning performance, Ivy thought with admiration. This is going to be a long week. While it wasn't beginning the way she'd thought, maybe she'd learn something from her mother. Ivy arranged a smile on her face.

Behind Carlotta, Mitch ambled inside. He wore a faded T-shirt with the arms shorn off and a pair of wrinkled sleep shorts. His hair stuck up at even odder angles than usual.

"Thanks for bringing Mom over," Ivy said to him as she stepped to one side and lowered her voice. "I know you have to be up early to open Java Beach."

"You could hear the screaming over the phone from the living room. I couldn't let Shelly deal with that." Mitch ran a hand through his hair. "Why did your cousin come so early?"

Ivy turned up her palms. "Someone confused the dates." Even though Diana didn't impress her as a pleasant person, she must have had a long day of travel. For a woman of her age and temperament, it couldn't have been pleasant.

Although she wasn't that much older than Ivy.

And Ivy had no idea where to put her.

Carlotta guided Diana into the parlor. "When is your mother arriving?"

"I thought she would be here with Robert. Mom barely speaks to me," Diana replied, her voice edged with indignation. She heaved a burdened sigh. "My flight was delayed, and I had to fend for myself at the airport. I couldn't find a single porter."

"How long has it been since you've flown?" Ivy asked. She hadn't seen many porters at domestic airports in years.

"Commercial or private?" Diana shot back.

"I've been trying to reach you for a long time," Carlotta intervened softly.

Diana dipped her head slightly. "I am terribly busy." Raising her chin, she shot a look at Ivy. "You told me I would have an ocean suite."

"And you will," Ivy said. "But not tonight." She pressed a hand to her pounding heart. No wonder her mother and this side of the family had been estranged for so long. How could her mother want to rekindle a relationship with such people?

While Carlotta and Diana settled in the parlor and talked, Poppy appeared beside her. "Need a nightcap?" She held a tray filled with several vintage brandy snifters. The crystal was old, even if the brandy wasn't.

Ivy shook her head. "It's late, and I have to figure out where to put Diana." It was past midnight now, and even the attic rooms were occupied by the sorority sisters.

Carlotta rose and approached Ivy. "Diana needs rest, *mija*. Is there a room for her?"

"I don't suppose we can put her on the couch."

"No, dear." Carlotta looked back at her niece, whose proud head was drooping with weariness. "I would give her my futon at Shelly's, but I fear she wouldn't be comfortable. And it's too late to call on Forrest or Flint. Are you sure every room is taken? It's only until the morning."

Ivy twisted her lips to one side. She could think of only one alternative, but she didn't like it.

As if reading her mind, Bennett leaned in. "Let's give her our apartment. I'll help you change the sheets."

Ivy shook her head. "I can't kick you out of your home."

"It's our home, and I think it's the only logical option given the time."

Carlotta smiled and hugged Bennett. "That's so generous. Thank you, my dear. I tell everyone you're like a son to me."

For a split second, Ivy almost wished he'd refused. "And where will we go?"

Poppy piped up. "Take my room. It's a little messy, but I can stay with Sunny. We'll bunk together anyway when the cousins arrive."

Ivy smiled at the offer. "I appreciate that, but I hate to dislodge you."

Bennett held up his palms. "How about the lower level? We'll be fine there until Paige opens the bookshop in the morning. I have a couple of brand new sleeping bags in the garage."

Ivy had to laugh at the absurdity of the idea. "Camping in my own house?"

Bennett slid his arm around her shoulder. "Think of it as practice for the great outdoors."

With a nod, she relented. "At least we'll be together." Thank heavens for Bennett and his go-with-the-flow attitude. At least they wouldn't be there long.

Working together, Ivy and Bennett tidied their unit and changed the sheets. She packed a small bag of toiletries and clothes, and Bennett did the same. They could dress in Poppy's room in the morning.

As they led Diana up the stairs, she continued complaining.

"I can't understand why you wouldn't have an elevator here." Diana slowed to spare her breath.

"This is a simple beach inn," Ivy told her, hefting her cousin's carry-on bag. Bennett had taken the heavier suitcases.

Diana huffed up the stairs, her turban slightly askew from the exertion. "It appears this was once a grand place. You've let it go."

Ivy reached the top of the stairs. "Excuse me?"

"It's under renovation," Bennett said quickly.

Ever the diplomat, Ivy thought. She appreciated that, because if it was up to her, she would put Diana on the couch. Immediately, she banished the thought. Was she becoming more like Shelly?

"It certainly needs work." Diana stepped into the apartment and glanced around. "The help usually lives over the garage. Not what I would call the best room in the house."

"That's right. It was the chauffeur's quarters." It was past two in the morning, and Ivy had reached her breaking point. Summoning a dose of faux cheerfulness, she showed her cousin to the bedroom. "I'm sure you'll be comfortable here. Ta-ta."

With as much flounce as she could muster, Ivy hooked her arm through Bennett's and steered him through the door.

Ivy was pacing the lower level when Bennett's footsteps sounded on the stairway.

As he cleared the last step, he dropped a pair of sleeping bags on the floor and grinned. "Ta-ta? First time I've ever heard you use that term."

Ivy folded her arms, feeling a little guilty about her reaction to her cousin. "I'm really trying, but even I have a little *ta-ta* in me."

Chuckling, Bennett swept her into his arms. "I'm glad you do."

She pushed back and planted a finger on his chest. "Are you patronizing me?"

"I wouldn't dare," he said, kissing her cheek.

"I'm trying to be a good host, but that woman is insuffer-able," Ivy said, pressing a hand to her forehead. Her emotions crackled inside of her like a flame that had suddenly ignited. "I can't believe Diana is related to us. If she's like that, just imagine her mother. I have new respect for Mom now. No wonder she kept us away from them."

"Diana certainly has a way about her." Bennett nodded toward the camping gear. "But now, let's get some rest." Within moments, he'd arranged chair cushions on the floor and unfurled the sleeping bags. "Your suite awaits."

A strange smell arose, and Ivy wrinkled her nose. "That's a weird smell." Together, they unzipped them and laid them flat so they could sleep together.

"This is new gear, although it's been storage a while." Bennett opened a couple of the high windows facing the beach.

The damp night air whisked through the openings, carrying with it the scent of the sea that usually instilled a sense of calm vitality in Ivy. But tonight, that would be more difficult. She pushed her hair from her forehead and sighed.

With a nod of understanding, Bennett took her hands. "We can pretend we're camping on the beach under the stars. Come on, sweetheart. You'll need rest to deal with your cousin tomorrow."

That was true. Yet, Ivy realized this wasn't all about her. "My mom will need a lot of support, too."

"We both have a busy weekend ahead. Clark and I will help Paige move so you'll have this room for the reunion."

Ivy flicked her gaze toward the bookshelves that lined one side of the lower level where they'd relocated the older woman's bookshop after the earthquake. "That's a lot of work. What about Mitch?"

"The weekends are his busiest days. We'll get some others

to help out. Brother Rip said he'd bring a couple of young surfers from the beach and put them to work."

Ivy nodded. "I'm going to miss having Paige here. It's going to be quiet this winter without her here."

"It's best that she's back in her shop."

"Paige is excited, too. She's ordered a fresh delivery of books." Ivy shivered in the night breeze. Aside from her newly acquainted cousin, she had a lot on her mind. The sorority group was leaving at the end of the weekend.

Bennett peeled off his T-shirt. Lifting the top sleeping bag, he slid in. "You look cold. Join me?"

Still wearing her shorts and T-shirt, Ivy eased in beside him. "This wasn't how I envisioned this evening ending."

Bennett wrapped his arms around her. "Surprises are the norm at the Seabreeze Inn. In fact, I'd be surprised if it was any other way."

"I work hard to make this place run smooth." Ivy didn't mean to sound defensive; she was just bone-tired. "Or as smooth as it can."

"You handle the unexpected well." He brought her hand up to his lips and kissed it. "And having excitement in our lives is good, even if it's a little inconvenient. Isn't this fun for a change?"

"I see your point." Ivy processed this, then raised herself on one elbow. "Are you calling our existence dull?"

His eye glittered. "Don't you want to get out and see more of the world?"

"Is this about our honeymoon trip?"

"Not specifically."

"You know I'm tethered to the inn for a while." Still, Ivy wished they could find the time soon. She would need it after the reunion.

Bennett enveloped her in his arms and kissed her. "Life has chapters, Ivy Bay. We'll get around to it. But let's not leave it until it's too late."

Her husband fell asleep quickly, though Ivy lay awake thinking about what he'd said. As important as the inn and the reunion were to her, she also had to make her marriage a priority. After all, they were happier together.

A PIERCING SCREAM jolted Ivy awake, and for a moment, she'd forgotten where she was. A deep voice rose against the sound of the waves. She lifted herself on their makeshift bed.

Another scream peeled against the early morning calm.

Beside her, Bennett flung off the covers. "That must be Clark." After grabbing his T-shirt and tugging it on, he sprinted up the stairs.

"Oh, my gosh. Diana." Ivy scrubbed her hands over her face. Bennett would deal with her cousin, who must have opened the door to a large, imposing stranger. Or Clark might have tried the door. People did that in Summer Beach, especially friends.

Besides, Clark was the police chief.

Ivy groaned. The sun was barely up, and already she had problems. But for this, she needed help. She grappled for her phone. Though she hated to disturb her mother again, this was another emergency. She tapped her phone.

When her mother answered, her words tumbled out. "Mom, I know I probably woke you, but I think you should get over here." Quickly, she told her what had happened.

"I'm already up with Daisy," Carlotta said. "I can leave her with Shelly. Mitch has gone to Java Beach, so I'll take one of the beach bikes and be right over."

"Thanks, Mom. You're the best. I realize just how good you are now. If Diana is like her mother, I can't imagine how you and Nana dealt with Maya."

"My sister was never easy, but she had her reasons. I'm sorry to learn Maya and Diana have problems, although I suspected as much."

After Ivy hung up, she drew a long breath, steeling herself against the inevitable. In the thin morning light that filtered through the high open windows, she blinked. She'd never seen the room from this angle, and it was sort of interesting. She was only a few inches off the floor on the chair cushions they had pushed together. Next to this seating area that they used for book club meetings stood a vintage wooden bar where the former owners had hosted parties during Prohibition, safely hidden from prying eyes on this lower level. The bar had beautiful inlaid burl wood patterns.

What's that? Brushing her messy hair from her face, she narrowed her eyes. A veneer end panel on the bar didn't look quite right. It seemed oddly askew. Maybe Bennett had bumped against it while he was arranging the bedding.

But she had little time to investigate.

Ivy rose to her feet and stumbled from the tangled bedding. Angling her head, she stared at the bar again. The veneer piece on the end looked a little different, as if it had been added. And it was loose. She gave it a good bang, and it shifted back into place. She'd deal with that later.

Just as she reached the first step, a thud sounded behind her. With her hand on the banister, Ivy glanced back. The thin side panel had fallen off the end of the bar. On the inside of the panel, a charcoal sketch of a woman taunted her.

What on earth was that doing there?

Ivy backed up and looked closer. It was a simple sketch of a woman whose hair was swept from her face, earrings framing the oval shape. But it was the eyes that intrigued her. With a flash of sudden recognition, Ivy stumbled back, her heart racing.

Oddly, the eyes mirrored her own.

Shaking her head in disbelief, she brought it into the light and leaned it against one of Paige's bookshelves before backing away.

Like the *Mona Lisa*, the eyes seemed to follow her every move.

Ivy pressed a hand to her forehead. Surely, she was imagining this. This piece and the subject looked more contemporary than the masterpieces she and Shelly had discovered earlier. The paper was simply tacked to the inside of a beautiful veneer panel. Although the artist was talented, the sketch was informal.

But what an odd place to store it, Ivy thought. As unnerving as this find was, she couldn't examine it right now.

Tearing her attention from the strange discovery, she raced up the stairs to rescue Bennett and Clark from her cousin. As the kitchen door banged shut behind her, she could hear Diana ranting.

"This man barged into my suite. You must call the police."

Ivy drew a breath to fortify herself. At this time of the morning, the smell of the ocean was thick on the foggy marine layer. Ivy charged up the stairs, huffing in the cool air. Bennett and Clark stood at the top just outside the door. Both were attired in T-shirts and jeans.

Bennett was trying to reason with her cousin. "Ma'am, this is Chief Clark Clarkson. He is the Summer Beach Chief of Police."

Diana pulled the collar of a quilted satin robe to her throat. Her hair was in frightful disarray, and her robe was tied at a haphazard angle. "I need the real police, not some beach bum pretender."

"Good morning, Diana," Ivy said, wedging between Bennett and Clark. "Clark is the police chief. And my husband is the mayor of Summer Beach. They had plans this morning, but we forgot to tell him we'd given you our place. A silly mistake, right?"

Diana backed away from the door. "This is ridiculous. You have the temerity to call this a luxury beachside inn?"

"We never say that." Ivy pressed her way inside. "We're more of a shabby chic sort of place."

"A what?"

Ivy stared at the woman, wondering where she'd gotten her unpleasant set of genes. With Diana's abrasive attitude, she could ruin the reunion even before her mother arrived.

That is, *if* Aunt Maya arrived. She'd better, Ivy decided. Especially after putting up with her daughter.

Granted, they had gotten off to an unfortunate beginning, but Diana was unyielding and judgmental. Ivy was flummoxed—what had happened to this woman to make her so bitter and imperious?

With a flash of insight, Ivy understood. Her mother yearned to reunite with her sister to put right whatever had gone so desperately wrong between them. That might have trickled down to impact Diana. If Carlotta had the chance to be a true aunt to Diana, how differently Ivy's cousin might have turned out.

At that, the lens through which Ivy viewed her aunt and her cousin tilted, and the chaotic situation shifted into focus. As compassion filled her heart, Ivy decided to try a more honest approach.

"We're of modest means, Diana, but we do want to give you the best we're capable of providing. My apologies for Chief Clark's friendly intrusion. He's a dear friend, and Summer Beach is the sort of town where neighbors tap on the door, and if it's unlocked, they might walk in. May we start over today? My mother is on her way right now. The two of you can enjoy coffee and breakfast on the balcony overlooking the ocean. You'll have a beautiful view. In fact, it's my favorite place to greet a new day."

Behind her, Clark added, "I'm sorry, ma'am. No harm was intended. May I welcome you to Summer Beach?"

As if struggling with how to react to kindness, Diana frowned at Ivy. "Since you're married to the mayor, I suppose the matter is settled. I take light cream and two sugars in my coffee."

"I'll send Mom right up. She'll want to hear all about how your mother is doing."

As the rising sun tossed tendrils of pink across the sky, Ivy backed out and shut the door. While it was early for this type of encounter, it wasn't the first time she'd had to calm an agitated guest. Still, her head was pounding, and every cell in her body was screaming to return to bed. But it was too late for that.

Clark gave her a thumbs-up, and Bennett put an arm around her. "Now who's the diplomat?"

Exhaling her tension, she leaned her head against his shoulder. "It's too early for this."

"Still, you were impressive," Bennett said with a grin. "Round one of the day goes to you."

Ivy managed a smile. "Let's hope the rest of the family tree bears sweeter fruit."

As she descended the stairs with Bennett and Clark, Ivy saw the silhouette of her mother on Shelly's bicycle. She wore a blue-and-white striped mariner top with white cotton pants and sneakers. Her hair was brushed into a ponytail, and she moved with youthful ease. That's what sailing would do for you, Ivy figured.

Bennett waved to her, then turned to Ivy. "I'll start the coffee."

"Thanks. And I'll make my sunrise omelets for Mom and Diana." It was going to be a busy morning. Ivy hoped Diana hadn't woken the sorority sisters. After last night, they needed to sleep in.

Carlotta swung off the bike and parked it by the kitchen door. After embracing Ivy, she nodded upstairs. "How is Diana?"

"Calmer, but I don't know for how long. I'm sorry I called so early, but I thought she'd need you this morning. How about sunrise omelets for you two?" That's what her mother called the sweet yellow pepper and avocado omelets she used to make when Ivy was young.

Carlotta turned into the brisk morning breeze off the water. "Thank you, *mija*. That sounds delicious—maybe a taste of her grandmother's home will calm Diana. Do you need help?"

"I'll manage. Your niece will want to see you." Ivy smiled at the thought of an omelet recipe that had traveled through generations of her family. What other traditions, habits, and lore did they share? She touched her mother's shoulder. "Was Diana always like this?"

"The apple didn't fall far from the tree. When we were younger, I thought Maya's attitude of superiority was merely because she was the oldest and the most fashionable. Part of it can be explained by her life experiences, but she has little reason to swan around like a queen now. And her daughter even less."

"Without her turban, she does look like Cruella de Vil," Ivy said, recalling what Shelly had called her. "I half expected to see a pack of Dalmatian puppies swarming around her."

Carlotta laughed. "Now, that's a funny visual. I'll have to conjure that when Diana tries my patience." She gazed up to the chauffeur's apartment over the stairway. "Evidently, she and her mother don't communicate well. Would you try to reach Maya again? I'm not having any luck."

"Even if it takes another pound of tiramisu, I'll talk to her."

Carlotta smiled. "That was clever of you. However, I'm glad Diana came early. We need to talk, to heal the past. I'd like to have her on my side to help bring her mother back into my life."

"I'm doing my best."

"I see that." Carlotta set her mouth into a determined line. "I believe almost anything is possible. The rest of it, we learn to accept." She pressed a hand on Ivy's arm. "I confess; I haven't told you quite everything, but I will. Older generations were more apt to sweep aside issues that we accept and speak about today. We'll talk later."

Ivy watched her mother leave to see Diana. Maybe Shelly was right about skeletons in the closet. Before returning to the kitchen, she visited her sister's garden to pluck the traditional fresh basil garnish for the omelets she'd promised.

Walking back, she spied Bennett and Clark inside the kitchen. They were talking and gesturing to the chauffeur's apartment. So far, Bennett had been a good sport about Diana, but she wondered if his patience would last through the entire reunion.

For that matter, she hoped her patience would last, too.

ennett filled the coffee maker and flipped a switch. Through the kitchen window, he could see Ivy in the garden, picking herbs for the breakfast she'd promised her mother and her cousin Diana. The sunlight caught the golden highlights in her hair. He watched for a few moments, transfixed as she moved gracefully through the garden. This was the woman he loved, and he'd do anything for.

Even cook for the entire brood, it seemed.

That's what Mitch had asked him about at Java Beach— and that's what he got for agreeing without paying attention. He grinned to himself. It wasn't so bad. He was happy to help Mitch make a good impression.

As the coffee brewed, he turned to Clark.

"Sorry about waking the household this morning," Clark said, easing onto a stool at the center island counter. "Although if I'd been an intruder, your guest might've scared me off. That's one tough lady."

"No worries. We needed to be up early for Paige's move. The rest of the guys should be here soon to help us pack. We'll start with the bookshop downstairs so as not to wake the guests. Once they're up, we'll pack Paige's personal belongings in her room."

"Noah and Piper will meet us at the bookshop to unpack," Clark added. "Piper offered to help Paige organize her private quarters."

Bennett pulled out a skillet and put it on the old stovetop. "They're doing a fine job of transforming the old airfield. The project should be complete next spring." He swirled avocado oil into the skillet.

"The park is a much-needed addition to the community," Clark said. "Children need a place to go besides the beach. Especially the older kids."

"Celia and Tyler have stepped up with support." The local couple had made a fortune in Silicon Valley in technology, and Celia ran the music program at Summer Beach's schools. "Tyler is personally overseeing a project to train and employ junior park rangers, which is what he calls the older teens who help organize activities and keep the grounds clean. It's a good program to give them experience and instill a sense of ownership in the project."

"And keep them out of trouble," Clark said.

Like any community, Summer Beach had a few kids at risk, and Bennett hoped this project would give them a new direction. "As it turns out, Tyler had a difficult childhood."

"I wouldn't have guessed that, what with all of his fancy tech friends from the Bay Area competing on who has the bigger boat."

Bennett's view of Tyler had recently changed. "We got to talking at the marina the other day. Seems his father died when he was young, and his mother struggled. He confided that he ran with a tough crowd as a kid until his mother met and married a wealthy investor. That's how Tyler managed to afford a top university. He told me he felt like an outsider though, like he didn't fit in."

Clark nodded thoughtfully. "So that's why he's been trying

to prove himself ever since. I grew up in a tough neighbor-hood, too. The truth is, I could've gone either way. But my mother insisted I attend college, and she helped me apply for scholarships. So, I studied music and law enforcement. It's obvious which way I went."

Bennett enjoyed learning more about Summer Beach resi-dents. Everyone had a story, and they weren't always what you first imagined. "Is that why I see you at all the music recitals?"

"It's my way of supporting the kids, even if I don't have any. Those kids have talent and dreams. Often I wonder how my life would have turned out if I'd pursued music instead of law enforcement."

"I've thought the same myself." The coffee machine gurgled to a stop.

Clark was quiet for a moment. "What dream did you give up on?"

"I played the guitar and sang a little. When I was a teenager, I thought I might be a rock star, like a lot of kids do." He poured two cups and put one in front of Clark. From one of the old twin turquoise refrigerators, he brought out eggs and cheese.

"So why didn't you pursue music?" Clark asked.

As Bennett drew out a cutting board and knife, he shrugged. "Probably the same reason you didn't. I didn't have the proper training, and I couldn't see a career path ahead. I had an uncle in real estate who seemed to enjoy what he did, and the flexibility appealed to me."

Clark lifted his cup. "And what made you run for mayor?"

"I grew up in Summer Beach, and I felt a responsibility to make sure the community retained its character. I didn't want to lose the village to fast food restaurants and chain stores." He placed a bowl and whisk on the counter.

So far, the community had avoided that, but Bennett knew the threat was ever-present. A few months ago, Summer

Beach could have lost the old airfield property to a discount mall developer had residents not rallied against it.

Bennett spread his hands. "Take Paige's bookshop, for example. A lot of small towns no longer have independent bookstores. To me, the idea of home isn't only about the house you grew up in. The concept of home also extends to the community and the people who make a town what it is."

"I hear you on that," Clark agreed, nodding. "When I go back to my hometown, it's grown so much that I get lost. I never needed a map when I lived there, but now I couldn't get around without GPS."

Bennett selected a ripe avocado from a large bowl on the counter and peered back at his friend. "Was the desire for that hometown feeling what brought you to Summer Beach?"

Clark grinned. "You're pretty smart for a mayor."

"Thanks, Chief." Bennett laughed. The two men had become good friends outside of their work for the city of Summer Beach. Sometimes they took Bennett's boat to fish, while other times, they played basketball on the weekends. For such a large, well-built man, Clark was fast and agile on the court.

Just then, Ivy burst through the kitchen door carrying fresh produce from the garden. She deposited the bright green basil, sweet yellow peppers, and a rippled heirloom tomato beside the sink.

Ivy pushed her hands through her still mussed hair. "What a way to wake up. I'm sorry you both had to endure Diana's wrath this morning."

"She reminds me of Darla." Bennett poured a cup of coffee for Ivy. "Crusty on the outside, but tender on the inside. At least, that's what I hope."

Ivy cradled the cup in her hands. "So do I. Honestly, it's hard to fathom that Diana is related to us. My mom is up there with her now."

Clark stood and pulled out a stool for her. "My apologies again for waking her."

Sensing Ivy's struggle, Bennett put his arm around his wife. "Relax, I can manage a few omelets."

Poppy hurried into the kitchen. "I heard the racket outside. What happened?"

Clark explained, "Your cousin was ready to call the police on me."

"Wow," Poppy said. "I can just imagine what your officers would have thought about that. Turning to Ivy, she added, "My room is all yours if you want it now."

"I could use a shower to clear my head," Ivy said. She looked at Bennett. "Are you sure you've got this?"

"Never better," Bennett replied. After Jackie died, he'd learned to cook for himself, and now he enjoyed it. Besides, he wanted to do this and more for Ivy. She hadn't slept well last night, and he suspected it was more than the discomfort of their makeshift bed.

THAT AFTERNOON, after moving Paige's belongings from the inn, Bennett stacked boxes by the bookshelves they'd arranged in the newly renovated space. He admired Paige's organization; she marked each box of books to correspond to a bookshelf. With plenty of help from Clark, Noah, and other friends, the move had gone swiftly, and all the bookshelves were in place. Pages Bookshop would be open for business tomorrow.

New shelves and beaded wainscoting were painted white, and nautical, navy-blue carpets were rolled over the restored hardwood floors. Axe Woodson's renovation team had salvaged the painted wood risers from the whimsical staircase, so the old book quotes were back in their former positions. The bookshop was fresh, clean, and inviting, yet it still retained the small-town charm that generations had loved.

And at the center of it all was Paige, looking excited over this fresh chapter in her life.

Bennett hoisted another box of books. "Where do these go?"

Paige gestured toward Piper, who was unloading cartons near the stairs. "That box goes over there in the local authors' section."

Piper was shelving books. "Those are probably the ones I've been looking for. Paige wants them right here." She brushed her fringe of short dark hair from her eyes.

"There's another one coming." Bennett was glad to see how well Noah and Piper were getting along. Two young people with such talent and shared love could have a wonderful life in Summer Beach.

He chuckled at his thoughts. He'd become more sentimental after falling in love.

Outside, Clark stood by the moving truck, stacking boxes on a hand trolley. When Bennett approached, he rested an arm across the top of the boxes. "I'm glad Noah brought his extreme sports buddies. We're getting too old for moving."

Bennett ran a hand across his neck. "We're just out of practice. Those guys are serious athletes."

He reached for a couple of cold water bottles from an ice chest and tossed one to Clark, then motioned to Noah, indicating he and Clark were taking a break.

Noah grinned. "We've got this. Nearly finished, anyway."

Clark eased onto a bench by the door, and Bennett watched the younger man take over. Noah had a good physique. While Bennett enjoyed running and staying active, he'd never been into extreme sports.

After taking a long swig of water, Clark leaned toward Bennett. "I heard old Charlie is taking bets on Noah and Piper at Java Beach."

"Not again. Do you think they know?"

"Noah might. He's the kind of guy who'd laugh it off."

"I'm not so sure about Piper. Think we should tell them?""

"You'd better let Noah do that." Clark raised his brow. "A while back, I had a serious talk with old Charlie about the line on Imani and me."

"No kidding? I didn't know you were that serious."

"She's not." Clark took a swig of water. "She doesn't like anyone talking about her private business. As for me, I'm biding my time."

Bennett nodded. "Patience will serve you, my friend."

JUST THEN, Piper called out to Paige across the room. "Where do you want this sketch of Ivy?"

Bennett looked up. Sure enough, Piper held a charcoal sketch. Although her hair was different, the eyes were perfectly drawn. "I've never seen that before. Where did this come from?"

"It was leaning against a bookshelf, so I packed it," Clark replied." I didn't really look at it."

"You can take that back to Ivy," Paige said. "It's quite good, so I'm sure she'll want it." She squinted at the corner. "That doesn't look like her signature, though. And what an odd mounting."

Piper turned the piece over, inspecting it. "It's a beautiful inlaid piece on the other side."

Paige turned her brilliant blue eyes to him. "Be sure to let her know we didn't mean to take it."

"Will do," Bennett said. He carried the piece to his SUV and slid it into the back.

*a*fter a much-needed shower in Poppy's room, Ivy dressed in a blue shirt with white clam-diggers. To elevate her outfit, she added a turquoise necklace and earrings her mother had given her. White sneakers with sparkly silver accents completed her innkeeper look.

She stepped outside on the patio, looking for Shelly. Since her talk with Carlotta, she'd been concerned about her sister. Shelly's usually ebullient personality—if sometimes edged with sarcasm—had been subdued since giving birth. Ivy understood that postpartum depression affected many women. Now she realized that Shelly hadn't been lazy or irresponsible on purpose. Besides caring for a new baby, she'd been suffering from depression and hormonal fluctuations.

Ivy felt terrible that she hadn't been more attuned to Shelly's needs, but she was thankful their mother had been.

She spied her sister in a shady part of the garden, surrounded by lacy green ferns and pink and blue hydrangeas. Shelly was on her knees, pulling weeds from beneath her plantings. A basket of cut blossoms sat beside her, and a baby carrier was nestled to one side. In it, Ivy could see Daisy clutching the neck of a small rubbery giraffe.

As her little niece cooed to greet her, Ivy bent down to sweep her hand across Daisy's silky hair. "Well, hello, sweetie. Are you helping your mom in the garden?"

Daisy's eyes widened, and a laugh gurgled in her throat.

"She sounds a little like you when she laughs," Ivy said, smiling at her sister.

"That's what Mitch says, too." Shelly tugged a weed from the garden and tossed it onto a discard pile. She clipped another flower for her bouquet. "The hydrangeas came back well this year. Even better than last year."

"They're stunning. Daisy seems pretty happy today."

"No meltdowns yet." Shelly sat back with her hands on her knees. "I heard I missed the skinny dipping party last night. Mitch says Java Beach is buzzing this morning over it."

Ivy groaned. "How did word spread so fast?"

"They were so loud they woke up Darla," Shelly said, tilting her head toward the cottage next door. "She was watching through the fence. Said it looked like they were having such a good time, she decided not to call Chief Clarkson on them."

Ivy put out her finger for Daisy to grasp. "That's a different Darla than the one we first met. Although, at one time, she probably would have been out there with them."

"Darla also said that Clark arrived early this morning." Shelly paused to clip a few dead leaves. "He had a scuffle with our newly arrived cousin?"

Ivy nodded. "I should just sleep late and let you fill me in."

Shelly laughed. "Seriously, what happened?"

After filling her in, Ivy nodded toward her apartment. "Have you met our cousin?"

"Oh, yeah." Shelly's eyes widened. "Mom called, so I went to meet her while you were in the shower. Diana reminds me of my eccentric clients from New York. Did Mom ever tell you why they were estranged?"

"She's vague about that. I suspect it had to do with their

other sister."

"Pilar. The way Mom talks about her, she was a brief bright light in their lives." She pulled another weed, then sat back. "I was thinking about all the good times we would have missed if we'd let one of our silly arguments get in the way. I hope that never happens between us."

"Me, too, Shells." Her sister's words meant a lot to her. "I'm sorry if I've been short-tempered lately."

"And I'm sorry if I've been out of sorts since Daisy was born."

"That was a big life change."

"But so worth it." Shelly smiled and tickled Daisy's feet. The baby laughed hysterically. "It's so funny, but she loves that."

"By the way, I noticed something last night when Bennett and I were camping on the lower level. Did you take a sketch from down there while I was in the shower? Or see one around?"

Shelly looked back at her with a curious expression. "No. Why?"

"I found one concealed in the bar in a really weird place." Ivy started to tell her about the eyes, but that sounded like a vain comment, even to her ears. Instead, she said, "It's old. No big deal. When Bennett and Clark were packing, maybe they put it somewhere."

Shelly's eyes brightened. "Do you think it's valuable?"

"I doubt it."

"Oh, well." Shelly shrugged. "Still, I wish we could get a big break sometime."

Ivy gazed up at the old house and smiled. "I think we already did." She turned to Daisy. "Going easy on your mother today?"

Daisy scrunched her face up as if to think about that.

After depositing the weeds she'd pulled into a bin, Shelly rocked back on her heels and removed her gardening gloves.

"I learned a few tricks from other moms in my support group." She paused, seeming a little self-conscious about her revelation. "Mom said she told you what was going on with me. I was afraid you wouldn't understand if I tried to explain it."

"Of course, I do. And it's not your fault."

Shelly shrugged. "I didn't know how to tell you."

"Why not?" Ivy asked gently.

Shelly rubbed her neck. "You thought I was shirking my duties around here."

"You'd just given birth," Ivy said, trying to sound more relaxed about that than she'd felt. "I wasn't expecting you to bounce right back."

Yet, even as Ivy uttered the words, a knot of guilt formed in her chest. She had thought that about her sister, although she hated to think of herself as uncaring. In fact, she often cared too much. Frequently, she had to remind herself that she couldn't—and shouldn't—solve everyone's problems.

But she'd missed the critical signs in Shelly.

Shelly covered Daisy's chubby, wriggling feet with a thin baby blanket dotted with yellow daisies. "That's about the millionth time I've tucked in your toes." She looked up at Ivy. "Have I been awful? Tell me the truth."

Her sister's words spiraled her guilt. What could she possibly say now? Ivy slung an arm across Shelly's shoulder. "I didn't mean to make you feel that way. Will you forgive me for not realizing what you were going through?"

Shelly leaned against her, turning from the sun flashing off the ocean beyond. "Even when we argue, I know it's because you want what's best for me."

"You can always count on that."

"Sisters forever?" Shelly grinned and hooked her pinky finger in Ivy's.

"Forever."

Ivy hugged her sister, just as she had when Shelly was a

child. Only now, that gangly younger sister was a grown woman—and now a mother—yet, she still needed her sister's love and support. That worked both ways with them, Ivy realized, recalling the moral support Shelly had provided when they'd moved to Summer Beach after Jeremy died.

Just then, a thought dawned on Ivy. "I wonder if Mom and Aunt Maya were ever as close as we are. Assuming Maya was capable of it."

"If they were, Mom must miss that."

That would be a great loss, Ivy thought. Beside her, Shelly was fidgeting with the edge of her shirt, and she sensed her need to talk. "Mom said you're getting some help. Do you want to talk about that?"

Shelly chewed her lip and nodded. "I scored pretty high on a post-natal depression test. In my group, I discovered what I've been feeling isn't so weird. It helps to be around others who've just had babies. We're all muddling through the haze together."

Ivy was glad Shelly had an outlet to express her feelings. "Being a new mother can feel awfully lonely. I wish I'd had that when Misty and Sunny were born."

"I didn't realize Daisy's babyhood would be so all-encompassing," Shelly said, wrinkling her brow. "Mothers don't get a day off. Even when Mom looks after Daisy, I still have to watch the time until I nurse her again. When I try to nap, I often wake feeling foggy. Now I know that's part of the process of your body trying to heal, but I had been so ashamed of how I felt. Like I was a bad mom for feeling overwhelmed." She grasped Daisy's fingers. "This tiny creature really blew up my chi and messed with my hormones."

At that, Daisy's face turned pink, and she let out a squeal and kicked off the blanket.

"Yes, we're talking about you." Shelly tickled her toes and tucked in the cover again.

They talked about Shelly's group and therapy sessions and

the changes she was making in her diet and exercise to try to regulate her body systems again.

Ivy nodded thoughtfully. "After Mom leaves, I can look after Daisy so you can continue." She would make the time for Shelly.

"I'd really appreciate that." Shelly looked relieved. "I've started yoga classes in the village." She held up a hand before Ivy could respond. "Teaching yoga here at the inn doesn't have the same benefit for me. Guests have expectations, and I need some *me* time. Poppy volunteered to teach our classes for a few weeks."

Mentally, Ivy dismissed what she might have said before she knew of Shelly's condition. Instead, she said, "I've heard that yoga is good for postpartum depression."

"For that, and a lot of other issues," Shelly agreed. "Still, I couldn't seem to drag myself to do it. But others in my group are going to this new yoga studio, so I'm committing to going almost every day while Mom is here." As she spoke, her face bloomed with hope.

A wave of guarded relief swept through Ivy. This was the best she'd seen Shelly look in a long time. "I can already see the difference in you."

"Really? I've barely started."

"You made a decision, and you're acting on it. That's a huge step."

Shelly beamed and hugged her. "Thank you for understanding."

At that, Daisy cried out and waved her arms, eager to join in. Shelly pulled away and brought Daisy into her arms and bounced her a little. "We haven't forgotten about you, Daisy-do."

Watching them, Ivy thought about her daughters. "When they're babies, it seems like that phase will stretch on forever. But they grow and change so quickly."

"I really want to enjoy Daisy at this age," Shelly said,

rubbing her child's back.

"And you will," Ivy said, hugging them both.

After a few moments, Shelly eased back. "I'd better nurse this little peanut before she gets cranky. I'll be in the downstairs powder room if you need me. Would you take the hydrangeas inside?"

"Sure." Ivy picked up the basket of flowers Shelly had clipped.

In her mother's arms, Daisy reached for the pink blossoms and laughed with an adorable, slightly crooked smile that melted Ivy's heart.

At once, Ivy recognized that expression. The child had her mother's easy, slightly off-sided grin that Shelly had since childhood. "Well, would you look at that," Ivy exclaimed. "She has your smile."

"How can you tell?"

Shelly couldn't see it, and Ivy laughed. But more important than that, Shelly's dark mood had parted, and a much-needed ray of hope shone through.

IVY CARRIED a vase of the pink and blue hydrangea blossoms Shelly had clipped for the foyer. When she approached the front desk, Poppy looked up. "Those are gorgeous."

"Shelly has done wonders with the garden this year." Ivy placed them on the table. "How is everything going?"

Poppy tapped her pen on the desk. "Beth just asked if she could stay on. Something about the airline changing her ticket. Shelly had told her about the reunion, but she said she wouldn't mind. In fact, she offered to film it for us as a favor. I thought some of the cousins could double up and give her a room."

"Are you sure she won't mind staying here during a family reunion? It's liable to get wild."

"As wild as the sorority sisters?"

"You have a point." Ivy passed a hand over her forehead. So far, that was the only skinny dipping party they'd had at the inn. "Thank goodness Beth wasn't injured. By the way, did all the ladies locate their swimsuits?"

Poppy grinned and shook her head. "We still have a couple in the lost-and-found. I think they went shopping instead. So, should I tell her it's okay for her to stay?"

Ivy considered this. "I was really looking forward to not tending to guests with the family around." Ivy had never closed the inn, so this was a rare exception that probably wouldn't be repeated for a long time. "We really need the rooms, and we already have our hands full with Diana. What if Aunt Maya and others are just as high maintenance?"

Poppy made a face. "I hope that doesn't run in the family."

"Would you call the Seal Cove Inn? They should have rooms opening up."

"That's probably better. I'll let Beth know and offer to help her with luggage if she needs it."

"Good. That's settled then."

Poppy picked up the phone to call the other inn while Ivy glanced at the room chart they'd made. Their family barely fit, even with some of the kids crashing on sofas at the homes of Forrest and Flint. They could do that here, too. *Too many Bays on this coast* was the family joke.

As much as Ivy was looking forward to the reunion, she would welcome the quiet afterward. The summer season had been their most profitable one yet, and Ivy had several ideas for more special theme weeks this winter.

"Sure, I'll hold," Poppy said, tapping her fingers on the desk.

Tomorrow was the end-of-summer beach party. Locals and tourists would gather on the beach with music, food, and games well into the night. A fireworks display would mark the end of the season.

Just then, Carlotta sailed through the door. "We need to talk about the activities for the reunion." She glanced into the parlor. "Before Diana joins us. When I left her, she was phoning her mother to see if she is coming with Robert. I've never seen a family that speaks so little to each other."

"Let's hurry then."

Beside them, Poppy shook her head. "Thanks all the same," she said before hanging up the phone. "There's a huge wedding party that's taking over the Seal Cove Inn."

Carlotta looked surprised. "Don't we have enough room for the family?"

"One of our guests needs to stay over." Ivy quickly explained. "Let's double up the boys. We can add a cot to one of the rooms."

Carlotta nodded with satisfaction. "Perfect. They won't mind."

"I'll give Beth a friends-and-family rate in advance," Ivy said. "For putting up with this crowd that's about to descend upon us."

"We have to keep them busy, so they stay out of trouble," Carlotta said. "I have a few ideas, but I thought you and Poppy would know more of what young people like to do. Let's sit in the parlor."

Poppy picked up a notepad, and they gathered around a table. "Everyone is arriving at different times, so we're planning to have appetizers available all afternoon."

"Burgers on the beach for a welcome party that evening," Ivy said. "We'll also have shrimp on the barbie and vegetarian options."

Carlotta tapped the table. "I'll find out what Diana wants."

"Mom, we shouldn't have to cater to her."

"If she were pleasant, you'd be the one offering."

Ivy was taken aback. "I suppose you're right."

"That's why I thought we should plan some games to keep

people occupied." Carlotta's eyes sparkled. "How about charades on the patio?"

Ivy agreed, and Poppy made a note. "Maybe a piñata for the kids?"

"We used to do that for birthdays," Carlotta replied.

Ivy chuckled at the memories. "I remember the time Shelly was blindfolded at her fifth birthday party. She swung at a yellow happy-face pinata with such vengeance, missed, and gave Flint a black eye."

"Scared me to death, but fortunately, he suffered only a mild concussion," Carlotta said, shaking her head. "Somehow, you all survived childhood."

"We could have a bouncy house for the kids," Poppy said. "Or maybe someone could dress up as a clown and make balloon animals."

Ivy laughed. "If I volunteered Bennett, I'd never hear the end of it."

"Or we can turn them loose at the pool or the beach," Poppy said. "Problem solved."

"That means I'll be on lifeguard duty," Ivy said. "Those boys get pretty rough."

"We can ask the older cousins to watch the children," Carlotta said. "Flint's clan has CPR and water rescue training. One year they used our old boat to sail from here to Vancouver, and he thought it would be a good idea. I believe you were living in Boston at the time."

Ivy didn't remember that. "I missed a lot of good years when I was gone."

"I'm sure you had many good ones in Boston," Carlotta said.

"I thought I did." Ivy made a face. "But if I'd known what Jeremy was doing on the side—"

Her mother placed a hand over hers. "Try to remember only the good now. The rest of it no longer serves you." Carlotta squeezed her hand. "Bennett is far different."

Ivy pressed a hand to her chest. Her mother was right. "I don't know where that came from. Sorry, where were we?"

"The beach," Poppy said, cutting in with a sympathetic smile. "And I like the charades idea, too. We should include some old-fashioned competition, like relay races. And a lot of the cousins play beach volleyball." She bent over her notebook to make notes on her schedule.

"Volleyball is an Olympic sport now," Carlotta said, stealing a look at Ivy.

To make sure I'm okay, Ivy thought. Just when she thought she was over the pain that Jeremy had caused her, old memories could crash back into her mind. Like now, when she has everything to be thankful for and good times ahead.

Another thought sprang to mind. Maybe that's the way it was for Shelly, too. Ivy recalled being listless, tired, and irritable after Jeremy died. She'd seen a therapist for her depression. The difference was that everyone expected her to be sad, whereas after having a baby, there was an expectation of joy.

"What do you think, *mija?*" Carlotta raised her eyebrows. "About the volleyball games. West Coast against East Coast. Or Bays against Reinas and everyone else."

"That should be fun," Ivy replied.

"Would you ask Bennett about playing his guitar around the firepit?" Poppy asked.

"Of course."

Just then, the front door squeaked open, and Ivy cringed. I have to oil those hinges before everyone arrives, she thought, adding that to her mental list. She was endlessly multitasking in her mind.

"Are we expecting anyone?" Poppy asked. "I didn't think the sorority sisters would be back from their shoreline cruise yet."

"Not that I know of." Ivy started toward the door.

Two young women wearing gauzy sherbet-colored sundresses burst through the door. "Surprise!"

10

*I*vy flung her arms around her eldest daughter. "Why didn't you tell me you were coming today?"

Misty ran a hand through her tousled brown hair and laughed. "Because then it wouldn't have been a surprise." She hugged her mother before turning to greet Poppy and Carlotta.

"And Elena, it's wonderful to see you, too." Ivy held out her arms to the other young woman, whose short brown hair framed bright blue eyes. A tiny blue diamond studded her nose, and a small tattoo of a flower peeked from behind one ear. "How is your jewelry business?"

Elena laughed. "It's been crazy busy. I loaned some pieces to the costume designer on Misty's new show. Misty wore them and posted photos to social media. Now everyone wants the same necklace."

"I had to practically drag her out of her shop," Misty said, making a face. "Her jewelry is more famous than I am."

"Your time will come, sweetheart," Ivy said. "Do you think the TV show will be extended beyond those first few episodes?"

"We all hope so," Misty replied.

Turning to Elena, Ivy asked, "Have you spoken to your mom and dad?" Ivy's eldest sister was Elena's mother, who lived in Sydney with her husband, Gabe.

Elena and Misty traded a guarded glance.

Carlotta cut in. "Are they okay?"

"It's just boat stuff with Gramps," Elena said with a slight shrug. "I'll tell you later, Nana."

"I'm sure the boat is fine," Carlotta said. "Your grandfather knows every part of that craft from bow to stern. Why, she's tight and yare, and bravely rigg'd as when we first put out to sea."

Misty stared at Carlotta for a moment as a slow realization lit her face. "Nana, are you testing me? I think that's a line from Shakespeare."

"Very good," Carlotta said, her eyes lighting with pride. "I see your education at Julliard wasn't wasted. But do you know which play?"

"His last...*The Tempest*, I think." Misty struck a theatrical pose with a hand on her hip. "'We are such stuff as dreams are made on. And our little life is rounded with a sleep.'"

"Excellent delivery." Carlotta clapped. "Bravo, my love."

While Misty gave a slight bow, Ivy inclined her head. "Where have I heard that phrase before?"

Carlotta's face brightened. "You might be thinking of *The Maltese Falcon*. For you youngsters, that was a classic film." She clasped her hands and raised her gaze. "Oh, that Humphrey Bogart had such a marvelous, deep voice, but he—or the screenwriters—changed old Will's line. Bogart said, 'the stuff that dreams are made of.' And so, it became."

"A lot of writers still mine Shakespeare," Misty said, nodding. "So much so that many of his lines have become cliches. I came across one in the last novel I recorded for an audiobook producer. I knew it seemed familiar, and it drove me crazy until I sourced it."

"I would love to see you perform again," Carlotta said. "How about a monologue or a soliloquy for the family?"

Misty wrinkled her nose. "Those cousins are a tough crowd. But I'd do a one-woman show for you, Nana. And Mom."

"What else do you have planned for the reunion?" Elena asked.

"Big surprises," Poppy said. "But you might want to practice your volleyball serve. You two will be on my team, by the way. Maybe girls against boys. Those East Coast guys won't know what hit them."

Ivy laughed at the idea, but she had her reservations, not that she didn't believe in Poppy and her team. "Don't rule them out just because they're into crew and field hockey. You might be surprised."

"Then we'd better start practicing," Misty said. She and Poppy and Elena high-fived each other, and Ivy laughed. Misty had spent part of a few summers with her grandparents, and with her height and lean, muscular build, she'd proved formidable in beach volleyball.

Just then, Sunny raced into the foyer. "Why didn't you tell me you were coming today?"

"Hey, you," Misty said, catching her younger sister in a huge hug. "I thought you'd be at summer school."

"I'm on break before the fall session begins. So, fill me in on everything that's happening in L.A. I'm so jealous that you're in with the cool crowd in Hollywood."

"It's not like that; I'm just happy to be working," Misty said, tucking a strand of hair behind her ear. "With this new show, I've taken a step up from theater and waiting tables, but I'm still investing in my career and taking acting classes. Hollywood is quite competitive, though the theater is still my first love. How is school going?"

"I'm still trying to decide what to do," Sunny replied, sounding a little unsure of herself. "I could have graduated by now, but I wanted to take more classes in hospitality. Maybe some other courses, too."

"I didn't know you liked school so much," Misty said.

Blushing self-consciously, Sunny ran a hand over her blonde mane. "Jamir has been encouraging me to figure out a real profession before I leave school."

So that's it, Ivy thought. She'd wondered why Sunny had stayed in school after she'd finally earned enough credits to graduate. Not that Ivy had a problem with that, but she wanted to know that Sunny had a plan. She didn't want her daughter simply putting off the inevitable task of finding work.

Ivy watched her two daughters, who were as different as they could be. She noticed a few changes in Misty. She'd cut her chestnut hair and added soft highlights. More than that, she spoke with increased self-assurance. Always the pragmatic one, Misty had studied acting and was truly becoming a professional. Ivy was glad that she was finding her way in what she loved to do.

Ivy wished the same for Sunny, who had been the spoiled, rebellious child, thanks in part to her father. Jeremy had always called her his golden-haired princess and showered her with gifts and an expensive private school education. Ivy didn't have a problem with the school—except that she couldn't afford it after Jeremy died—but their father was quick to lavish gifts and cash on his daughters instead of spending time with them. Ivy had taken issue over that with Jeremy, and after his death, Sunny had difficulty facing the new reality of their economic situation.

Recalling how she'd had to bring Sunny back from Europe, Ivy thought about the moneyed, fast crowd she'd been running with. After racking up enormous charges on Ivy's credit cards—including a first-class return ticket from Europe she'd bought without Ivy's knowledge—Sunny had reluctantly moved to Summer Beach. Ivy insisted she finish school in Southern California. Fortunately, Jamir—her friend Imani's son—was studying pre-med at the same university and seemed to be a positive influence on her.

Suddenly, she wondered, could there be anything more between them?

The girls' laughter interrupted Ivy's thoughts. Seeing how animated and happy they were, Ivy was glad that her mother had insisted on this reunion. Keeping in touch with family—especially in person—seemed difficult when everyone was going in a different direction. Still, it was important that they got to know their extended family outside of texts and social media posts.

Yet, Ivy worried about Aunt Maya's grandchildren, who were more privileged. She had no idea what sort of attitude they would bring to the reunion. Judging from Diana and Robert, she was bracing herself. Would Sunny be able to handle the one-upmanship she'd had trouble with before?

Laughter rose from the young women, and Misty elbowed Poppy. "I have an idea of something we could do at the reunion. Want to hear it?"

Poppy grinned and picked up her notepad. "Aunt Ivy, do you mind if we chill at the pool and talk about it?"

"Go ahead. The sorority sisters won't return until late. And Shelly should be finished feeding Daisy soon. I'll send her out to see you all."

"I can't wait to see how much Daisy has grown," Misty said.

"By the way," Ivy added. "We're full right now—and our cousin Diana has taken the chauffeur's apartment. Would you and Elena mind sharing rooms with Sunny and Poppy?"

"Sure, Mom," Misty replied. "I was planning on that anyway."

"That'll be fun," Elena said, and Misty nodded.

"Oh, dear," Carlotta interjected, drawing her fine, dark eyebrows together. "Diana told me this morning that her brother Robert and his wife will be joining us after all. I forgot to mention it."

"And Aunt Maya?"

"Still undecided, I'm afraid."

Ivy considered that and wondered what else she could do. "We'll figure it all out."

She and Bennett might have to continue sleeping on the lower level in their makeshift bed unless they could move Diana into another room. Finding places for guests that fit their needs was always a challenge when they were busy. At least with family, she could suggest they share rooms. Ivy thought about the vacations they'd spent with other family members when she and her siblings were young. Bunking together was often half the fun.

Misty and Elena picked up their bags, and the four young women left, talking and laughing as they caught up on news and gossip.

"You and Shelly and Honey used to be just like that," Carlotta said. "Having everyone together will be wonderful. Thank you for arranging this reunion, *mija*."

"I'm happy to do it, and I certainly haven't managed it alone." Seeing the gratitude in her mother's eyes was touching, and Ivy thought about how she might feel in her mother's position. One day, the fates willing, she hoped to have grandchildren as well. Although that day would be far away, she imagined. Misty and Sunny were still making their way in the world. At their ages, she'd already been married and become pregnant with Misty.

With a start, she realized she could be a grandmother. Was she really that old?

"Mom, what does getting older feel like?" Ivy blurted out the words before she'd even had a chance to think about them.

Carlotta laughed. "What a funny question. Although children often ask me what it feels like to be old. I prefer the word *mature*, of course."

"What do you tell them?"

"That I don't feel any different inside. I like to think I'm a little wiser. And as long as I keep moving, I can maintain a level of fitness, although that can go quickly if I don't keep it up."

"You and Dad get good workouts on the boat."

"We do a lot of walking in port, too. Most of all, the work is in here." Carlotta touched her heart. "If you keep your spirit young, you can still summon joy." Tilting her head, she added, "I would imagine people still mistake you for Misty's sister, especially with your fresh new hairstyle. Are you beginning to feel your years?"

"Not usually. I just thought about what I was doing at Misty's age. I'd made you a grandmother by then."

Carlotta smiled. "Honey has the distinction of being first with Elena, but I know what you meant. Is that what concerns you?"

"I just never thought of myself that way. Not yet, anyway."

"It can be surprising, but I think you'll welcome the day when it comes. Though some people don't—maybe it's hard to accept the fact that we're not forever young. As some women—and men—lose their bloom of youth, they worry that their spouse will find them less desirable. But I think fascinating people remain perennially attractive, and they make much better company. Especially to themselves."

Ivy laughed at that. "It's good to enjoy your own company."

"And staying curious keeps one vital and sharp."

"Maybe Diana needs more curiosity."

"Now there's an idea," Carlotta said.

Ivy was quiet for a moment. "You sound as if you've seen it all."

"There isn't much that surprises me anymore." Pausing, Carlotta placed a hand on Ivy's shoulder. "Yet, that doesn't mean we can't still keep our sense of wonder. Throughout the ages, most of the great scientists and artists have shared that. It's easy to become hardened as old arteries, but fight against that with everything you've got."

"A sense of wonder," Ivy repeated. "I'll remember that." As she embraced her mother, love and appreciation welled within her. "I hope I gain as much wisdom as you have. And for the record, you'll always be beautiful, inside and out."

A LITTLE LATER, Ivy sat in the library, tending to her bookkeeping. Her mother had gone to help Shelly with Daisy.

Ivy left the French door slightly cracked for fresh airflow from the ocean. She could hear laughter from the pool where Misty, Sunny, Poppy, and Elena had gathered. While she worked, she liked hearing the sounds of people having a good time. Besides, when anyone was at the pool, her training made her aware of how fast accidents could occur. She liked to make sure guests in the pool area were safe.

Laughter broke out again. Whatever those four had in mind for reunion activities was sure to be fun and appeal to the young cousins, so Ivy trusted them to surprise her. She would enjoy whatever they planned, too.

Still, she'd be happy simply drinking a glass of wine by the fire pit, digging her toes into the cool sand, and breathing in the fresh sea breezes.

She smiled to herself. Ideally, with Bennett by her side, talking about the day they'd had.

She never tired of that.

Ivy was almost finished with her bookkeeping entries when she heard the sorority sisters return from their coastline cruise. The house was soon filled with friendly chatter and laughter.

Ivy loved hearing the activity of a full house, inside and out. People were enjoying themselves, and as an innkeeper, what could be better than that?

"Five more minutes," Ivy said to herself as she neared the end of the expenses she was entering on the computer. Book-keeping wasn't her most exciting task, but she had learned to do it to run the business. Actually, it wasn't so much different than when she'd managed her household budget, except that she tracked it on the computer now.

The inn was finally showing a small profit, even after salaries for her, Shelly, and Poppy, along with Sunny's part-time work. Staying on top of their expenditures and fore-casting revenue from their reservations helped her manage the cash flow needed for special events and repairs.

Through the cracked door, Ivy heard footsteps, then chairs scraping against the tile on the patio outside.

"I want to talk to you about the DNA results I received."

With her fingers poised above the keyboard, Ivy paused. The voice was low but unmistakable. *It's Shelly.* But who was she with? It had to be their mother. Ivy reached for another cash expense receipt to enter. She was glad that Shelly was telling Carlotta about the test she and Mitch had taken for Daisy.

"I appreciate you referring me to that company for the tests," Shelly said. "However, I'm concerned about the accu-racy. I think they should run the tests again."

That's odd. There was a pause, and Ivy turned to hear better. Not that she was eavesdropping...or rather, she didn't mean to.

"Did you find something you didn't expect?"

Ivy sucked in a soft breath. *Beth.* She lowered the receipt to the desk.

"It has to be a mistake."

"That's what people usually think at first."

Another pause.

"Well, I just don't see how it would be possible."

Ivy leaned to one side in her chair, struggling to hear better.

"Look, if there were no surprises in DNA ancestry results, I wouldn't have a show on television."

Ivy closed her eyes, intent on following the conversation.

"It gets worse," Shelly said. "When I was looking at the results online, I got an email from…that person."

Shelly added something Ivy couldn't quite make out, but she could tell her sister was agitated. Ivy felt a twinge of guilt for listening, but she couldn't help that they sat where she could hear them.

"She wants to meet me."

Ivy could hear the anguish in her sister's voice. Sensing trouble ahead, she passed a hand over her face. Shelly didn't need this on her mind, especially in her current state.

"When?"

"As soon as possible."

Another brief exchange ensued that Ivy couldn't make out, followed by a long pause.

"Let me guess," Beth continued. "You discovered a half-sibling."

Ivy almost cried out. She clamped a hand over her mouth. No, she thought, willing Shelly's answer.

"What? That would mean my dad—and he would never… Or my mom, and I really don't think…but I don't know…"

"Who else?"

Leaning farther toward the crack in the door, Ivy suddenly lost her balance and crashed onto the floor. The antique rug softened her fall, but she couldn't help emitting a little cry when she hit her shoulder.

"What was that?"

Shelly had heard her. Ivy lay on the floor, trying not to make a sound, but her shoulder began throbbing. What a stupid mistake, she thought, chastising herself.

"Let's walk by the ocean," Shelly said softly. "I don't want anyone else to hear this yet."

11

*P*oppy swept into the kitchen with a basket of blueberry muffins left over from breakfast. "Do you need me anymore, Aunt Ivy? Misty, Elena, and Sunny want to buy supplies for the reunion this morning. I'll be back before the sorority sisters check out."

"Go on, spend some time with your cousins," Ivy replied.

The group was checking out today, except for Beth, who was staying over. After overhearing the conversation with Shelly, Ivy was having second thoughts about her.

Poppy put the muffins down on the center island where Bennett was reading the local news. "See you later."

Ivy wiped her hands on a dish towel and turned to Bennett. "Fresh muffins, half price."

"Don't mind if I do. I ran a couple of extra miles this morning with Clark." He tapped the Summer Beach community newspaper on the counter. "Did you see this article? The family reunion made the paper."

Usually, Ivy would be pleased with the coverage, but a growing sense of unease gathered around her neck. "What does it say?"

Bennett began reading. "A combined family reunion will

be held at the Seabreeze Inn, where relatives from the Bay and Reina families will gather from across the country. Carlotta and Sterling Bay are visiting from their around-the-world sailing voyage, and they will depart after the reunion."

Ivy's heart fell. What if someone—whoever Shelly had been talking about—saw this? Immediately, she stopped herself. No one would know about this unless they lived in Summer Beach.

Or were visiting. Shelly did say the person wanted to meet.

Bennett smoothed his hand over hers. "Hey, what's wrong?"

"It's nothing."

Bennett raised his brow. "Sure seems like something to me."

Ivy shook her head, even though she knew she wasn't very convincing. He could always tell when she was out of sorts. But she wasn't ready to share this potentially explosive issue. At least, not until she spoke to Shelly and got some straight answers.

What sort of mess had her sister stumbled upon? Or could it simply be a mistake?

Instead, she said, "I'm a little on edge with everyone arriving for the reunion."

Although Bennett looked doubtful, he acquiesced to her. That would give her time to pull the story out of Shelly and start damage control before the reunion was underway.

Bennett stretched. "Are you planning to move Diana into another room today?"

"As soon as I can. Shelly is coming to help while Mom looks after Daisy. We have a lot to do today after checkout."

"Do you need some help?"

"It's a lot of work to clean and change every room. Poppy will help when she returns, but Shelly will need to leave earlier." She was still nursing Daisy, so she couldn't be away from her baby too long. Bennett usually had a full schedule between his mayoral duties and his real estate business. "If you have time, I'd really appreciate it."

Bennett swept his arms around her waist and kissed her cheek. "While camping downstairs has been fun, if it means moving back into our place, I'll be there. I promised my sister I'd go to my nephew's ball game. That shouldn't take long. On the way back, I'll pick up the supplies from Nailed It for those repairs you wanted. I'll see you soon."

BY THE TIME SHELLY ARRIVED, Poppy had returned and was checking out the departing guests. Ivy and Shelly climbed the stairs to start cleaning rooms. Ivy wanted to move Diana as soon as possible.

While Shelly swept the floor, Ivy polished the antique furniture with an orange oil formula Shelly had made.

"About your DNA test," Ivy began.

"I don't feel like talking about that," Shelly mumbled.

"But I think we need to." Ivy had replayed in her mind the conversation she'd overheard, and she needed to know more.

Shelly just shrugged, which incensed Ivy. Surely her sister realized the gravity of the situation. Or she'd decided to ignore it, which would only make it worse.

Holding the orange oil aloft, Ivy whirled around. Despite her concern for her sister's condition, she couldn't hold back. "Shelly, I know something has happened, and you need to tell me."

Shelly clutched the broom and shifted uneasily. "I only did the tests for Daisy's sake."

"Is that really all you have to say?"

Shelly narrowed her eyes. "What exactly do you think you know?"

"I overheard your conversation with Beth."

"You were listening?" Shelly's question took on an accusatory tone.

"Not intentionally," Ivy replied. "I had left the door in the library ajar for a little fresh air, and you sat down and spilled everything to Beth. I had no idea what you two were going to talk about."

"That was you? I thought I heard something. Why were you listening to our conversation?"

"As if I could help it. What was I supposed to do? Inform you that I was listening? The point is, you're in touch with someone who is purporting to be part of our family."

A glum expression shrouded Shelly's face. "The DNA doesn't lie. Beth explained it all to me."

A thought flashed through Ivy's mind. This is what Beth did for a living—producing the *Family Archives* segments for television. "That's why she's staying, isn't it? To film your meeting with this person."

"What? No. Beth can't get a flight. Or maybe she just likes Summer Beach and wants to stay longer. She offered to film the reunion for us. I told her I would pay her, but she wouldn't hear of it."

Ivy put her cleaning supplies on the bureau. "Think about that, Shelly. Why do you think that might be? You're the savvy New Yorker here." She folded her arms. "Don't be so naïve. Beth smells a story."

Shelly looked away and sighed.

"So, let's hear it."

Her sister slid a side-eyed look at her. "You just said you already heard it."

Exasperated, Ivy threw up her hands. "I couldn't hear *everything*." She glared at her sister as she rubbed her shoulder, which was still sore from her fall. Finally, she took the broom from Shelly and sat on the bench at the end of the bed. "Will you start from the beginning?"

Blinking, Shelly bowed her head. When she spoke, her voice was barely above a whisper. "I wish we'd never had that test done."

"Look, I know you're miserable over this. But I can't help if you don't tell me. And this secret is tearing you up inside. I can see it on your face, Shells."

When her sister didn't reply, Ivy hesitated. She'd thought about this last night, so she'd hardly had any sleep. She had to ask the question, although the answer might forever change her feelings. Yet, sooner or later, the truth would come out.

Drawing a deep breath, Ivy uttered the words she dreaded, "Do you think it was Dad?"

Shelly shook her head.

Ivy breathed out. But she wasn't finished. "Not Mom?"

"No."

"Then we don't have an unknown sibling floating around out there?"

"Not us…"

"Then, who?"

Inching her way toward Ivy, Shelly tugged a strand of hair from her bun and twirled it around her finger. "I don't know how to explain it. I really don't understand all that DNA stuff. I mean, there's a chance, I guess, but it's probably slim."

Trying to stay calm for Shelly's sake, Ivy gestured for her sister to join her on the bench. "Just try your best."

Shelly perched on the edge as if poised to flee. "Not long after I set up the profile on the ancestor website, I got an email. From a woman who says she's related to us. She's been doing research."

Ivy pressed a hand against her forehead. This wasn't just a theory; there was a real person out there. "Where does she live?"

Shelly raked her teeth over her lower lip. "On Crown Island."

"That's awfully close."

Ivy and Shelly exchanged sober looks, and Shelly nodded.

Crown Island was a short ferry away. As Ivy tried to piece

together the puzzle, she leaned forward, her elbows on her knees in thought. "So, was it our grandpa? Or Grams?"

"I'm not sure what happened." Shelly pressed her hands against her face. "Beth asked her team to trace the family."

"Mom needs to know about this."

Shelly darted a look toward Ivy. "So, how are you going to tell her?"

"Me? You're the one who discovered this."

"I can't, not by myself," Shelly said in a small voice. "I feel so conflicted over this."

Ivy's heart went out to her sister, and she took her hand. "We can tell her together."

Shelly wrapped her arms around her torso. "Honestly, I'm a little scared."

"If it's the truth, then we need to."

"That's worse. I can't hurt her now. This is supposed to be a happy reunion for her."

"It still can be." Between this news and Aunt Maya, Ivy feared her mother might be facing more than she'd planned. "When will Beth have more details?"

"I don't know," Shelly said. "Maybe we can wait until after the reunion."

"That might work. This new information is sure to be a shock. Still, Mom might welcome the truth."

This was the last thing Ivy wanted to deal with during the reunion. She was trying to see both sides, but it wasn't easy. A part of her still wanted to have it out with her sister. After all, she'd warned her, hadn't she?

Her face scrunched with worry, Shelly rocked back and forth. "About this new person—I have no idea what she's like."

"By person, you mean relative. We might as well call her that." Ivy sighed. "We should meet her first."

Shelly nodded reluctantly. "Do you think Mom will accept her?"

"I have no idea." But their mother had a strong sense of fairness. "What if this new relative is after something from us?"

"You mean money?"

"Wouldn't be the first time," Ivy replied. The thought of that settled heavily on her shoulders.

"I'm really sorry," Shelly said, wiping a tear from her eye. "I never dreamed anything like this would happen."

Seeing her sister's distress, Ivy reached out to embrace Shelly. For better or worse, they shared a bond. She stroked Shelly's mussed hair, soothing her. "I'm sorry for what I said. You couldn't have known about this. But I promise we'll get through this together."

As for how they would tell their mother, Ivy had no idea. At least their father would be arriving soon.

IVY AND SHELLY finished cleaning the upstairs guest rooms, including the master bedroom that Paige had stayed in these last few months. They gathered sheets and trudged downstairs to deposit them in the laundry room. Ivy had a part-time worker who did the laundry twice a week, and she would be in shortly.

As she neared the laundry room, Diana appeared in the hallway. In an imperious tone, she said, "I'm glad I caught you, dear. I'm going shopping in the village. Please have my bedding changed and my room cleaned before I return. I'll only be gone an hour, so see to it right away." She took Ivy's hand and pressed a folded bill into it.

Ivy was so shocked at her cousin's actions that she was at a momentary loss for words.

Shelly laughed. "Diana, you're actually bribing your cousin?" She looked at Ivy's still outstretched hand. "If so, that will take more than a couple of dollars."

"Well, I never—"

"No, I'm sure you haven't," Ivy said, cutting her off. She tucked the sheets under one arm. "We're moving you to another room, Diana."

"There's no need for that. I'm perfectly happy in that suite. Although you should have an elevator. And there are clothes in the closets and bureau drawers that should be removed because I need the room." She turned to leave.

"Those are my clothes," Ivy said. "And my husband's."

"Be that as it may, they must still be moved for guests."

Ivy's patience was growing thin. "Our other guests have checked out, and we have a room in the house for you now."

"Does it have an ocean view?"

Ivy wished she'd never mentioned that. "Yes."

Diana considered this. "However, I do enjoy the balconies and the living room, so I will stay where I am. You can put Robert and his wife in that other room."

"We have another room for them," Ivy said, trying to remain calm.

Diana heaved a great sigh. "I am not moving."

Ivy heard the taps of heels behind her.

"Why, Diana, your mother would be ashamed of you," Carlotta said. She passed Daisy to Shelly, who quickly dropped her armload of sheets in the hallway. "Preferring the chauffeur's quarters." Carlotta laughed lightly and took Diana by the arm. "I promise I won't let that get around. Come with me, and I'll show you the room we have for you. Ivy, what was the number?"

Ivy quickly told her mother which room. "It's Imani's old suite."

Before their mother steered Diana away, Shelly added, "And since we're a shabby chic sort of place, we don't offer that daily change of sheets you wanted. We'll leave your tip on the dresser."

Carlotta gave Diana a reproachful look. "You didn't."

"I would do that in any hotel," Diana said, lifting her chin in defiance. "My maid changes my linens daily."

"*Ay-yi-yi,*" Carlotta said, chastising her niece in a scathing string of Spanish.

Ivy nudged Shelly. "Let's get out of here."

She and Shelly, along with Daisy, hurried to the powder room off the ballroom. Ivy had found a vintage fainting couch downstairs and fashioned a white cotton slipcover to fit it. She'd added a few of her hand-painted pillows and a soft, rose-hued rug to brighten the space. With a chandelier, a parquet floor, and a mirrored vanity, it was a quiet, well-appointed spot for Shelly to tend to Daisy. Guests could use another bathroom on the other side of the ballroom.

Even Daisy squealed at Diana, and Shelly cooed to soothe her. "We'll never let Cruella de Diana bother you, little one."

Once Shelly was settled on the couch with Daisy cradled in her arms, she turned her face to Ivy. "I have something else to confess."

Ivy pulled up a chair next to her. "What's going on?"

"An email came through today from the woman I told you about."

"The one that contacted you about a DNA match?"

"That's right. She wants to meet. Even though Beth arranged the DNA service, and I know she'd like to film the meeting, it doesn't feel right to me. I'm a little nervous."

"Why is Beth so insistent?"

"I might have promised her an exclusive."

"*What?*"

"I didn't think it would amount to anything. It was the standard form her assistant sent over."

"For what?"

"The DNA search."

Something didn't feel right to Ivy. "Is this why you did the search through her? To be on her show?"

"No, I swear to you. She made it sound so easy, saying her

staff would take care of handling the tests for us. I thought she was sort of a friend. A professional friend, that is."

"Also known as a client or acquaintance. Do you have the paper you signed?"

"It's in my email."

"Send it to me, and I'll ask Imani." Ivy drew a hand across her forehead. "We'll deal with this issue when we have to, but for now, let's act as if everything is fine. This reunion is supposed to be a fun, joyful occasion."

Shelly smiled with relief. "You're the best, Ives."

"We'll figure it out together." As if this weren't enough, Ivy still had to get their Aunt Maya here, and Diana was clearly not helping. Maybe Carlotta could make some headway today.

Ivy grinned at Shelly. "Once you're finished with Daisy, let's crank up the music and get this job done."

One crisis at a time, she decided.

12

*A*fter attending his nephew Logan's off-season ball game to raise funds for a children's hospital charity, Bennett stopped by Nailed It to pick up supplies for his project at the inn.

Since Ivy was so busy today, Bennett had also promised to pick up lunch for everyone. After chatting with the owners, Jen and George, he paid for his materials and walked a few paces to Java Beach.

When Bennett pushed through the door of the coffee shop, the scent of fresh coffee and beach reggae music filled the air. Doors stood open to the patio, and every table was filled with people talking over lunch. Business looked good.

Mitch raised his hand in greeting. "Got your order ready for you." He motioned to his employee, another young surfer with the same sun-bleached hair as Mitch. "Hey, Ace. Would you get the mayor's order? It's in the fridge. And add a dozen of those cookies that are cooling on the rack."

Mitch turned back to Bennett. "I made two kinds of salad and put in several croissant sandwiches. Plus, warm chocolate chip cookies. You'll have plenty of food."

"You're the best, thanks." Bennett was relieved that Mitch was in better spirits today. "Are you ready for this reunion?"

"Yeah, I guess. For Shelly's sake, I decided to chill and roll with it. No one can say anything to me that I haven't heard before. And I survived that."

Bennet bumped Mitch's fist. "Good attitude."

"The only thing I'm worried about is that someone might make a snide remark to Shelly. I don't want to see her hurt. Their cousin Diana thinks pretty highly of herself. She's a wild trip, that one."

"You've met her?"

"Not exactly. But you just missed them. Carlotta brought her here for coffee and dessert. They didn't stay long. It sounded like it wasn't Diana's kind of place."

Bennett grinned. "So, what did she have to say?"

Looking sheepish, Mitch ran a hand across his frayed Grateful Dead T-shirt. "Actually, I saw them coming, so I hid in the back and sent Ace out to help them. I've got a couple of new shirts for the reunion, but this one wouldn't make the best first impression, know what I mean? I want Shelly to be proud of me."

"Can't blame you." Bennett glanced at the crowd in the coffee shop. Darla was in the corner with her glittery visor, talking with Louise from the Laundry Basket down the street.

Mitch nodded toward her. "Think it's okay if I bring Darla to the reunion? She's been hinting about it, and after all, she's like family. I'd feel bad about her watching the party from next door and feeling left out."

Darla had practically adopted Mitch and doted on Daisy as if she were her own grandchild. "I'm sure it will be fine. What's one more person?"

"Cool. She'll really like that."

Ace brought out several bags of food and passed them across the counter to Bennett. "Here you go, man." The young guy nodded toward the ocean. "I hear you surf."

"A little," Bennett said, grinning at Mitch. "Maybe I'll see you both out there." He bumped fists with them and left.

He stepped into his SUV and placed the food on the seat beside him. Ivy was expecting him, and he suspected that now, more than never, she needed his support. He started the car and turned toward the inn.

When Bennett entered the house, he heard music blasting from upstairs and the sounds of laughter. Climbing the stairs, he called out.

A flurry of sheets billowed into the hallway, and he jumped to one side to avoid the mound of linen.

Ivy poked her head out. "Oops, didn't see you there." She glanced at the bags he held. "Lunch is here," she announced.

"Woo-hoo," Shelly cried. "We're starving. Only Daisy has had anything to eat—at my expense, of course."

"That's called being a mom," Ivy said.

Bennett laughed. They were in good spirits. Even though keeping up a house of this size with guests coming and going could make this beach haven into a madhouse, he wouldn't have it any other way. He had to remember how fortunate he was.

Poppy bustled from the guest room, and Shelly followed with Daisy, nestled into a stretchy cloth wrapped around her shirt.

"We'll take those," Poppy said, scooping the bags of food from Bennett's hands and heading downstairs.

When Ivy came out of the room, Bennett swept his arms around her. "How's it going here?"

"Pretty good. My old room is ready to go for Aunt Maya if she comes. We'll have all the sheets and towels washed later today for the rest of the rooms. By tomorrow, we'll be ready for the next wave." She pressed a hand to her forehead. "Having everyone check in and out at the same time makes for a huge job."

Bennett brushed tendrils of hair from her flushed face.

Even hot and tired, his wife was beautiful. "We'll be back in our little nest by tonight, so you can relax in your own bed."

Ivy smiled. "You, too. You've been a good sport."

"Hey, I knew what I was getting into. This is anything but boring."

Ivy laughed at that. "You missed the blow-up with Diana. She wanted to continue staying in our quarters. Fortunately, Mom swooped in, set her straight, and whisked her away."

"They turned up at Java Beach."

"Oh, my gosh. Did Mitch meet her?"

Bennett laughed and told her what had happened.

"Shelly will be relieved. She's a little worried about introducing him to the family."

"She shouldn't be. Mitch is an honest, hard worker. And he's running a successful business. Can't argue with that." Still, Bennett knew that Mitch's prison record could be a juicy piece of gossip if Aunt Maya heard about it. Instead of mentioning that, he kissed her on the forehead. "Let's eat, and I'll make those repairs afterward."

Ivy gazed up at him. "Tonight, let's enjoy a quiet night if we can. Once the rest of the family begins arriving, it's going to be wild around here."

"How about I fire up the barbecue on the beach later? I'll throw something on, and everyone can gather around the firepit."

"That sounds perfect," she said. "We have burgers in the fridge."

As they made their way downstairs to put out the food for lunch on the patio tables, Bennett thought about how much he looked forward to meeting the best of the Bays and Reinas. Difficult people didn't bother him—he had to work with all sorts of personalities at City Hall. But he was concerned for Ivy and Shelly. They were working hard to entertain a large crowd of people. He hoped that Diana was the only sour apple in the barrel.

Still, he sensed that sparks would fly before the end of the event. But wasn't that half the fun of a reunion?

After they'd all finished eating, Bennett remained with Ivy on the terraced patio. Poppy left to make a phone call, and Shelly had gone to rest. Suddenly, he remembered the sketch in the back of his vehicle.

"I meant to tell you that we inadvertently picked up a sketch of you and carted it off to Paige's. I've got it in the SUV."

"So that's where it went," Ivy said. "But I've never seen that before. I found it downstairs." She told him how she'd discovered it. "It's certainly not of me, though. I would guess that it's something Amelia stashed away. Still, the resemblance is kind of uncanny."

Bennett rubbed his chin. "Amelia Erickson sure was creative in her hiding places. And that sketch looks a lot like you." He touched Ivy's face, gently lifting her chin to the light. "Especially the upper part of your face around the eyes. Wait here; I'll get it from the garage."

"I'll come with you."

When Bennett reached the garage, he opened the back of his SUV and brought the sketch into the sunlight. "We can get a good look at it here." He stepped back. "That's an amazing likeness. Can you tell anything from it?"

Ivy leaned in. "Judging from the fullness in her face, the woman was young—likely a teenager. Her eyes hold such joy." She held up a hand. "No, more than that. *Love.* As if it were the happiest day of her life."

"You must have a doppelganger from history. Any idea who it might be?"

"None at all." Ivy shivered and rubbed her arms. "Likely, it's a coincidence."

Bennett put his arm around Ivy and drew her to him. "Amelia left a lot of mysteries in her wake." But this one was the strangest yet, he thought. The resemblance was uncanny.

Except for the old-fashioned hairstyle, it might have been Ivy.

"Let's put it in the parlor and see if anyone notices it," Ivy suggested with nonchalance.

"Tell me where you want it."

Bennett picked up the sketch. He could tell Ivy was uneasy about this, and he knew she wouldn't stop until she had answers. Maybe her mother would have some insights.

"I'll bring an easel from my art studio."

"Show me which one you want. I can carry both."

One thing Bennett had learned about Ivy since they'd been married was that she didn't ask for help very often unless it was a task she couldn't physically manage. Her first husband had traveled a lot, so she must have had to manage everything herself. That was endearing to him, but he'd quickly learned to offer his help.

Only when it was necessary, though. That had required of period of adjustment on his part. Admittedly, he was still working on it.

"Are you sure? I can get it."

Bennett grinned. "Just tell me which one." When she started to protest, he added, "I'm not one to let my wife do the heavy lifting, even if I do find her independence wildly attractive. A man still likes to be the man."

"And what a man." Ivy broke into a smile—that dazzling, genuine, somewhat self-conscious smile that got to him every time. She walked ahead of him.

He strolled behind her, the sketch tucked under one arm, admiring her graceful gait. His heart still pounded at the sight of her.

"That one," she said, nodding at an easel in the corner.

Bennett gave her a little kiss before he picked it up. "Let's go, Mrs. Mayor."

Laughing, Ivy guided him toward the parlor. "Right there, so it can be seen from the foyer. That way, no one can miss it."

Bennett started to offer possible solutions, but instead, he restrained his instinct. As a man—and the mayor—his nature was to rush in and solve problems. However, he'd learned that some situations he viewed as problems resolved themselves given patience and time—and other people's ingenuity, which often exceeded his own.

He wasn't the central character in this theater of life. Other people had challenges they needed to work through, and solving everyone else's dilemmas didn't necessarily serve them. Still, giving a hand or offering words of encouragement were important, whether among friends, family, or the community.

Ivy would figure this out. He was learning to trust her process, although that was still easier to say than practice.

Bennett set up the easel and positioned the drawing with its wooden backing. Admiring it, he stepped back and put her arm around her. "I know you'll find some answers to this."

Ivy rested her head against his chest. "I hope so. I wish I could figure out how to appeal to Aunt Maya, too."

He kissed her forehead. "I'm sure you will, sweetheart."

"Thanks for saying that." As Ivy gazed up at him, a slight smile curved her lips.

Once again, she melted his heart.

13

*S*itting in the library early the next morning, Ivy left voice messages again for Aunt Maya and Robert. She doubted they would return her calls.

Ivy tapped on the desk, thinking. She was running out of time to reunite her mother and her sister for the reunion.

Frustrated with the lack of communication, she searched on her computer. *Bespoke travel services.* She would pay for a ticket if she had to, but more than that, she needed Aunt Maya's commitment.

Short of booking a flight and landing on Aunt Maya's doorstep, Ivy was at a loss as to how to reach her aunt. Her cousin Diana was no help with her mother; she seemed intent on enjoying a holiday at the beach. Diana's brother Robert was also unresponsive.

According to her cousin, the Italian delicacies and Carlotta's offer of meeting in Italy seemed to have started the thaw, but Ivy needed to finalize plans right away. She wondered what else she could do.

"Travel concierges…" Ivy perused a few websites until she finally found one that sounded personal. "VIP Concierge Travel, same day service. Okay, Ms. Tracy, let's see if you can work your magic on Aunt Maya." She tapped a phone number.

By the time she got off the phone, Ivy let out a guarded sigh of relief. The traveling concierge agreed to visit Aunt Maya in person today as well as arrange the ticket, and provide a limousine to the airport. If her aunt agreed, of course. All Ivy had to do was to leave a message for Robert, asking him to tell his mother, and send a telegram directly to Maya informing her of the same.

Unless Robert and Maya answered their phones, that was the best she could do. Sunny had told her that younger people didn't take phone calls much anymore. They only texted or responded to emails. But Maya wasn't of that generation. For that matter, neither was Robert.

An hour later, Ivy was still in the library responding to reservations on the computer and comparing them against next year's schedule of special-event weeks. When her mother walked in, she peered over her new red-and-zebra-print readers. "Hi, Mom. What's up?"

Carlotta rested a hand on her shoulder. "I'd like to buy more fresh flowers for the house at Blossoms. Will you come with me?"

"Shelly usually takes care of that from her cutting garden. Did you see her flowers?"

"They're lovely, but I have something else in mind."

"You could tell her what you'd like."

"She's so busy with Daisy. And I think you need to take a break."

"Really, I have to finish here." Ivy was hoping to hear from Tracy, the travel concierge.

Carlotta peered at the screen. "Next year can wait. We need to talk."

Ivy knew that tone; her mother's suggestion was anything but that—and she already had her purse looped over her arm. Carlotta would not take *no* for an answer.

Ivy saved the document and took off her glasses. "Shall we walk or take my car?"

"We'll need to put the flowers in the back seat."

Carlotta turned and started toward the door, leaving Ivy little choice but to follow. She'd been summoned. She made sure to tuck her phone into her pocket in case that VIP call came through.

On her way out, Ivy plucked her white denim jacket from the coat stand and slipped it over her navy T-shirt, giving it a quick half-tuck in the front of her faded jeans. She knew her mother always liked her to look presentable, as she called it, even if she didn't say it. This was the best she could do and keep up with her mother's determined stride.

This was serious.

Ivy pulled her vintage Chevrolet convertible from the garage, put the top down, and opened the door for her mother.

"Thank you. What a beautiful sunny day." Carlotta gathered her white cotton eyelet skirt and slid onto the leather bench seat. She drew a pair of sunglasses from her purse.

Ivy eased the car from the driveway. "You didn't summon me to talk about the weather."

"No, dear. It's about Maya."

Ivy waited. Just then, her phone buzzed, but she couldn't answer it.

"She actually called me. It seems she received a telegram about a travel concierge who is coming to see her today."

"I sent that. Will she see her?" Ivy held her breath.

"She will, although she's not sure she can make the flight." Carlotta turned to her. "But thank you for trying. I didn't even know you could send a telegram anymore."

"You can find anything online, Mom." If Maya didn't make it, her mother would be very disappointed, and they'd be stuck with Diana.

"Even if she doesn't come, maybe we can begin to settle

our differences and work our way back to each other," Carlotta said. "But it's you and Shelly I'm concerned about now."

"Why?"

"No one is perfect. But I'm afraid that Diana might overhear you and Shelly talking about her. Old houses have ears."

"Thin walls, you mean."

Carlotta lowered her sunglasses and pursed her lips. "I mean, we have a lot of family arriving. Now, I'm the first to admit that Diana's behavior has been brusque and heavy-handed, but that's her way of protecting herself. When she acts superior, it's as if she's building a protective wall around her. Can you understand that?"

So that's what this was all about. Ivy let out a breath. "I can. Have we been behaving badly?"

"It's one thing to talk about someone when they're thousands of miles away, but you were raised better than how you're acting toward her. She's been through a lot, perhaps more than we know."

"Has she said something to you?"

"She doesn't need to." Carlotta huffed with indignation. "Although it's been a long time since we've seen each other, she's still my niece."

"I'll do my best, Mom. Even if she tries to woo me with a tip into changing her sheets every day."

Carlotta put a hand over her face and shook her head. "Well, you are justified. But please do what you can. Especially if her mother arrives."

"Sounds like they need a reunion of sorts, too."

"I'm afraid you're right. Still, let's be civil and loving. This is family, even though they're difficult. Let's see if we can unite and have fun."

Ivy sighed and took this in. As much as she hated to acknowledge that her mother was right, she was. And Ivy felt a little embarrassed over their treatment of their cousin. "I'm so sorry, Mom. We didn't mean any harm, but the humor got away from us. If we crossed a line, I apologize."

"Good. I understand that should work both ways, but it probably won't. We have to take the high road." Carlotta pushed her sunglasses back up on her nose. "I'm sure you'll also understand why I don't want to repeat myself with Shelly."

"I'll relay your message to Shelly and Poppy, just to make sure."

"If you remember nothing else, treat your elders with respect. They've often been through more than you can imagine. Even the foolish ones."

"Excuse me? Diana isn't that much older."

"I'm also speaking about Maya. They might be far from perfect but remember that their years are limited. And everyone has regrets. Even you, I'm sure. We don't need to keep reminding them of the past. Who should have called, who said what, and so on. Perhaps I'm as much to blame."

"I've had plenty of regrets, so I understand," Ivy said, feeling justifiably corrected. Growing up, she and her siblings knew that when Carlotta was quiet and firm, that's when they really had to change their behavior. *Or else.* Forrest had been grounded so many times they'd all lost count. "I promise I'll do better, Mom."

Ivy pulled the car to a stop beside the flower stand. Imani was wrapping a bouquet of roses for a customer. In her vivid cotton print sundress and dark braids wound into a crown on her head, she was as bright and cheerful as the flowers that surrounded her.

Carlotta patted Ivy's shoulder. "Thank you for understanding. Now I can relax and have a wonderful time with my family. And your father will be here as soon as he can get a flight."

"Did he manage to get a ticket?"

Carlotta gave her a hopeful smile. "He's still working on it, but I'm sure he'll manage. Even if he misses the reunion, he promised to come for Shelly and Daisy."

Ivy's heart sank a little. She'd hoped her father would be here by now. "I wish Honey and Gabe could join us, too. But I understand. This is a chance for them to take the boat out on their own."

They got out of the car, and Imani greeted them. "What would you like today?"

Carlotta put her arm around Ivy. "The most cheerful bunch of flowers you have."

Imani gestured to a bright section of sunny yellow, pink, and orange blossoms. "These are pretty uplifting."

An older, elegant woman in pressed denim and a crisp white shirt with a jaunty scarf approached them. "Why, Carlotta Bay, is that you?"

Carlotta turned around. "Ginger Delavie, it's so good to see you."

While the two women spoke, Ivy pulled Imani to one side and lowered her voice. "I'll make this quick. Shelly has a situation with a former client who's here in town. The woman— Beth—produces a reality show, *Family Archives*, and Shelly thinks she signed something waiving some rights about a search, which wasn't Shelly's intent. Would you mind talking to her right away? The woman offered to film the reunion as a favor to Shelly."

Imani arched an eyebrow. "*Family Archives?* I watch that show sometimes, but it can get awfully gritty among family members. I doubt that's who you'd want at your family reunion. She and her staff are known for setting up people, and they've been sued a lot."

Ivy groaned. "Can you please help Shelly? I'll make it worth your while."

Imani waved her hand. "I make enough from this flower stand and my new online shop to take care of my friends. I'll talk to her later today."

While Carlotta and Ginger finished speaking, Ivy and Imani picked out some floral combinations.

After her friend departed, Carlotta turned back to them.

Ivy held up a bouquet of blossoms. "What do you think, Mom?"

"That's just what I had in mind. Those pink roses are Maya's favorites. It's funny I recall that, even after all these years."

Ivy prayed her mother's hopefulness wasn't for naught.

They finished selecting flowers, and Imani wrapped them up. As Ivy was loading them into the car, her phone pinged again.

"Oh, my gosh, I almost forgot." Quickly, she pulled it from her purse. "Hello?"

It was Ms. Tracy, the travel concierge. "I'm calling to say that I'm here with your aunt, and she has agreed to go to the reunion in Summer Beach. I'm staying to help her coordinate some outfits and pack. The limousine will pick her up tomorrow. I'll send you flight details when we hang up. I'm happy to say your mission impossible is mission accomplished."

Ivy let out a little squeal. "You're a miracle worker. Thank you so much!" From the eager look on her mother's face, Ivy didn't care what this cost. Her mother's happiness was priceless.

When she hung up, Carlotta clasped her hands to her heart. "Is she coming?"

Ivy embraced her mother. "Maya will arrive tomorrow."

Just in time. Ivy let out a sigh of relief. Now, if only they could sort out the DNA mess as well.

14

*I*vy stood with her mother and Bennett at the San Diego airport, waiting for the flight the concierge had arranged for Maya.

"That's her," Carlotta said, waving to a taller, more angular version of herself. She clasped her hands to her chest in anticipation.

Ivy put her arm around her mother, who was quivering with excitement. Carlotta's eyes were bright with emotion. Seeing the joy on her mother's face was worth the effort Ivy had put out. She only hoped that after all these years, the reunion wouldn't prove a disappointment.

While they waited for Maya to reach them, Ivy wondered how the rift between the two sisters had grown over time. She couldn't imagine being estranged from Shelly or Honey.

As Maya neared them, Carlotta held her arms wide. Joyful tears glimmered in her eyes. "Maya, *mi hermana*."

Her sister choked out a single word, "Carlotta."

For a moment, the two women stared at each other, searching for the familiar and willing the years to fall away. In an instant, they fell into each other's arms, the past a memory and the future theirs to create.

With Bennett standing next to her, Ivy was overcome by what this meant to her mother. She was eager to hear more family stories, especially about Pilar, the middle sister.

On the drive from the airport, Carlotta and Maya sat in the back seat of Bennett's SUV, catching up on what time had stolen from them. This was the aunt Ivy hadn't seen since she was a very young girl, and she was surprised at how different Maya was from her mother. While Maya was a little older than Carlotta, she seemed weary, not only from the trip, but from life in general.

To Ivy, watching the long-estranged sisters greet each other had been like opening a journal to her mother's life, with a view to a past that Ivy had almost forgotten existed. She had expected the tearful reunion, but what lay ahead intrigued her even more.

"Do you remember visiting Summer Beach?" Carlotta asked Maya as Bennett turned onto the main road. "Papa brought us here one time."

Peering from the window, Maya grew quiet. "I never thought I would return. It has changed little." Her aunt's voice trailed off, and she seemed lost in another thought.

"We've tried to retain the community's original character," Bennett said. He turned onto the beachfront lane in front of the inn.

Ivy touched her aunt's hand and nodded toward the grand old home. "Welcome to the Seabreeze Inn, Aunt Maya."

Bennett drove past the front of the home. Shelly's seasonal profusion of summer flowers, from blushing pink to riotous reds this year, lined the front walk. Towering palms stood guard at the entryway, swaying in the ocean breezes.

Maya's eyes widened, and her face paled. "This is your inn?"

"We're in the process of an ongoing renovation," Ivy replied, nodding. "We like to call it shabby beach chic. Shelly has done wonders with the garden, and the former owner left some priceless antiques that came with the house. You'll have her lovely suite, which has an incredible view of the ocean."

Blinking, Maya touched her forehead. "What was her name?"

"Amelia Erickson," Ivy replied. "She and her husband Gustav were art collectors from San Francisco."

Maya pressed a hand to her mouth. "I had no idea... I don't know if I can stay here."

Confused, Ivy looked to her mother, but Carlotta looked just as perplexed. "We've taken extra care to make the room comfortable for you. It's quite cheerful."

"Perhaps it is." Maya squeezed Carlotta's hand. Nevertheless, the color drained from her face, and she stared at the house, sadness pooling in her eyes.

Ivy couldn't imagine what was going on in her aunt's mind. What had come over her?

Bennett turned into the car court behind the main house. "I'll take up the bags if you'd like to make your aunt a cup of tea."

"That's just what we need," Carlotta said, patting Maya's hand. "Traveling can be exhausting. We also have fresh squeezed orange juice. We can sit on the patio and take in the sea air. It's quite invigorating."

"I'll tell Diana you've arrived."

Maya stepped toward the sketch Ivy had discovered, her attention riveted on the drawing.

"You found it," Maya said, her voice barely above a whisper.

Ivy touched her shoulder. "You've seen this before?"

Maya drew a breath and nodded. "Not in many years." Her expression melted with compassion. "It looks so much like her."

"Who is that, Aunt Maya?"

But Maya only shook her head.

Carlotta crossed the parlor and stood beside her sister.

Together, they gazed at the sketch as if entranced. "Is it really her?"

Maya nodded. "Ivy favors her a great deal. I noticed the resemblance at the airport. She has her eyes."

"It's Pilar, isn't it?" Ivy gestured at the sketch that captured her expression. In art classes, she had attempted a self-portrait. Drawing her own eyes had been the hardest part for her.

Shelly and Poppy stepped into the room, looking quizzical at the somber mood.

"Pilar was our middle sister." Maya smiled sadly at the young woman whose image gazed back at them through time.

"Where did this piece come from?" Carlotta asked.

"I found it downstairs," Ivy replied. Quickly, she explained how she'd discovered it.

Maya gazed at the portrait. "I was there the day he began drawing."

Carlotta looked perplexed. "I don't know who you're talking about."

"No, you wouldn't. Times being what they were." Maya raised a hand and let it fall as if that explained everything.

In studying the portrait, Ivy saw such an expression of love in Pilar's eyes. She turned to her aunt. "You met the artist?"

Maya pressed a hand to her chest as if a secret so great constricted her ability to breathe. "It was her young man. Flavio."

Ivy peered at the signature. "I can't make out the name very well."

"Flores."

Carlotta tilted her head. "Flores de…?"

Maya nodded. "Bourbon. The families were quite close in Spain. You were probably too young to recall much."

Sadness washed across Carlotta's face. "He must have been devastated, too. Did he return to Spain after the accident?"

"He did," Maya said.

"Were they engaged?" Ivy asked.

Averting her gaze, Maya hesitated. "A marriage was out of the question for them due to prior commitments."

"Poor Pilar." Carlotta kissed her fingertips and pressed her heart.

Shelly looked between her mother and aunt. "I'm not following any of this. If that's your sister, what is her sketch doing here?"

"Amelia was a collector and patron of the arts," Carlotta said. "I imagine she acquired the piece. Yet it seems sad that it was here all this time; I know our mother and father would have loved it to remember Pilar."

Shelly was right. This explanation didn't make sense to Ivy either. "But Aunt Maya, you said you were there. You knew Flavio. After Pilar died, wouldn't he have kept the sketch or given it to your parents?"

"Maybe he needed the money and sold it to Amelia," Shelly said.

"Oh, no. Nothing like that." Maya's face flushed, and she reached to a chair for support. "I must rest now."

While Carlotta helped her sister up the stairs to her room, Ivy threw a look at Shelly and Poppy. "Aunt Maya knows something she's not sharing." She approached the sketch and leaned in, searching for answers or clues. "What are you hiding, dear Pilar?" The eyes gazed back at her, and a sweet smile curved her lips but revealed no secrets.

"Maybe we're approaching this all wrong," Poppy said. "What information would an older sister conceal to protect a younger one?"

"You might be onto something." Ivy turned toward Shelly, who was fidgeting with the edge of her blouse. "What secrets would I have kept from you—fifty years ago?"

"You have to consider the family, too," Poppy said. "They were very traditional."

A thought occurred to Ivy, but before she could speak, Shelly blurted out, "I have to check on Daisy."

Ivy watched as her younger sister darted from the parlor just as Maya had. She stepped closer to the sketch and picked up the board the paper was mounted on.

"Where are you going with that?" Poppy asked.

Ivy shifted it onto her hip. "I want to take a closer look at Pilar, and the light is better in my studio."

Poppy trailed her and helped move an easel to a bright window open to the sun.

Ivy picked up a magnifying glass and pulled up a stool to inspect the sketch, the thick paper, and the decorative veneer board it was mounted on.

Poppy hovered nearby. "What are you looking for?"

"I don't know. Something that looks unusual. I'm trying to think as Amelia would have."

"It's a shame that an accomplished woman like her deteriorated in the clutches of Alzheimer's," Poppy said. "I've read that science is making advances now."

"That's right. But it wasn't only her disease." Ivy peered closer. "The war affected her on a psychological level. Think about how she rescued the masterpieces in the basement and offered sanctuary to others in her attic. Amelia grew accustomed to concealment and was committed to helping people."

"Do you think she knew Pilar?" Poppy asked.

Ivy recalled what her aunt had said when she arrived at the house. "I don't know. But I think she's been here before. A long time ago, maybe when it was Las Brisas del Mar."

"That would mean she knew Amelia."

"Maybe." Ivy paused with the magnifier in mid-air. "Or maybe my grandmother knew her. Both were accomplished and active in the Southern California community."

"Did she ever say anything?"

"I was so young I wouldn't remember anyway. Even so, I believe Maya is hiding something."

"She doesn't seem malicious." Poppy eased onto a stool beside her. "What if she thinks it's something that would hurt the family? This might be like Pandora's box."

"You mean, once opened, it might unleash revelations we'd wish we didn't know?"

"It's possible."

Shelly appeared at the doorway. "What are you doing with that sketch?"

"Taking a closer look." Ivy turned. Shelly hadn't been gone long. "How's Daisy?"

"Still asleep. For now, anyway." She took a step forward. "What were you saying about Pandora's box?"

"I'm convinced Maya has been here before." Ivy told Shelly what their aunt had said in the car. "I think this sketch has a history she's not sharing."

"Or she's not quite ready to," Shelly said. "Sometimes people don't know how to talk about sensitive topics."

"Especially if they've been keeping a secret for a long, long time," Poppy added.

Shelly coughed into her hand. "And if it might affect other people."

"That's a real consideration." Ivy angled the sketch toward a shaft of bright light and examined it under the magnifying glass. A heart-shaped pendant or locket with an engraved rose hung from her neck. But there was something else. "Well, what do we have here?"

Poppy and Shelly leaned in.

Ivy pointed to a faint line. "The pencil dust has gathered there for some reason. Maybe something brushed on top of it, but I have another idea. There's a razor blade and a sharp knife in my tray. Would one of you bring them to me?"

"On it," Poppy said. In a flash, she was back, carefully wielding the sharp instruments.

Using extreme care, Ivy slit an edge of the thick paper that was affixed to the wood. She slid the flat blade under the old paper until she felt something. Working carefully, she coaxed out a corner of a paper. Faint writing covered one side.

"Is that the provenance?" Poppy asked.

Ivy glanced at it. Pilar's name was at the top. Under it was another brief entry. "More than that, I think." She stood and tucked the note into her pocket. "I'm going to get some answers."

Shelly sucked in a breath. "I'll go with you. I can bring Daisy."

"Me, too," Poppy said.

Ivy shook her head. "Let's not overwhelm Aunt Maya. But I promise to tell you everything." She still had to pass on her mother's stern advice, too. "Mom wants us to show Diana and Aunt Maya more respect. They've been through a lot that we might have misinterpreted."

Shelly and Poppy traded sheepish looks and nodded in agreement.

IVY CLIMBED the creaky wooden stairs to her old bedroom, the one that had once been Amelia Erickson's, too. As she lifted her hand to knock, she recalled the strange shadow she'd once seen in the room and wondered if Maya would sense a presence there.

Ivy lifted her chin. Not that she believed in that sort of thing, but she was willing to admit that some people might be attuned to such things. Her mother certainly was.

Still, she had an inn to run, and if something like that got out... Besides, she had more important questions for her aunt. She tapped on the door. "Aunt Maya, may I come in?"

Carlotta opened the door. "Come in. Maya is resting," she said quietly.

Her aunt was leaning against the decorative pillows Ivy had positioned against the headboard. "Is there anything I can bring you?" Ivy asked, acutely aware of her mother's eyes on her.

"No, dear. But I'm glad you're here." Maya patted the edge of the bed. "Do sit down."

Ivy glanced at her mother, and she nodded her approval. As Ivy eased onto the white duvet she and Shelly had arranged, she sensed an energy in the room. But it wasn't Amelia; it was a heaviness, a burden, that seemed to surround Maya.

"We've been talking, *mija*." Carlotta sighed. "We missed so much in these past years."

"It was my fault." Maya folded her hands in her lap. Her eyes contained a deep sadness. "I have something to share with you, Carlotta. It's probably better with Ivy here."

Carlotta sat next to her sister and smoothed a hand over her shoulder. "Whatever it is, I'm here for you. If you're ill—"

"Nothing like that." Maya grasped Carlotta's hand. "Many years ago, I swore to my mother that I would protect you. And our family honor. I was already married, but you were young. We couldn't risk telling you."

"I don't know what you're talking about." Carlotta drew her brow together. "We had no secrets in our family."

When Maya hesitated, Ivy spoke up, "You've been here before, haven't you?"

"Yes, I have," Maya said. "But we're jumping ahead in the story." She picked at a thread on the duvet. "Carlotta, you were too young to understand. But when Flavio visited with his mother, he and Pilar fell in love. Our parents separated them, and Flavio returned to Spain. He had a duty, a marriage that was already arranged."

"In the portrait, I could see the love in her eyes," Ivy said.

Maya nodded. "They had a great love and continued writing to each other. Before long, Flavio returned to California to look for her. I was the one who told him where she was."

"What do you mean?" Carlotta asked.

"In those days, young women were usually sent away for..." Maya raised a hand and let it drop. "Pilar was pregnant. Our mother knew Amelia Erickson, so she asked if Pilar could stay here. In those days, pregnancy was a stain on the entire family. That would have ruined our youngest sister's chance of marriage."

Carlotta's lips parted with surprise. "I never knew she was pregnant."

Yet, that made sense to Ivy. "Amelia had helped others during the war and after."

"Amelia Erickson was a brave woman who didn't care what anyone thought of her," Maya said. "I only met her once, though it was rumored that she was suffering from dementia. Her devoted staff ran the house and looked after her and her guests. It wasn't unusual for Amelia to take in visitors for extended periods of time."

In listening to Maya, Ivy was beginning to see her aunt in a new light. Her mother had been right. "Were there other girls here?"

"Only one that I knew of," Maya replied. "I wasn't supposed to know where Pilar was, but I overheard a conversation between our parents. I missed her so much that I just had to see her. And I wasn't the only one."

The years melted from Maya's face as she spoke, and Ivy was transported into the story. "Flavio was with you?"

"He was desperate to see her. Oh, he was so handsome, and he loved her so much. I picked him up along the way, and he showed me the ring he'd bought for her to propose." Guilt-ridden over her revelations, Maya looked down. "I drove the new car Papa had given me for my birthday. The convertible."

Carlotta drew in a sharp breath and passed her hand across her forehead.

"That day, we sat on the patio in the sunshine, and Flavio sketched Pilar." Maya smiled wistfully at the memory. "I left them alone, and when I returned, he had proposed. I'd never seen Pilar look so happy, though I knew our parents would be furious. Flavio was engaged to a young woman from a very important family. Their fathers were in business together, so Flavio's father and Papa had both been quite dismayed."

Maya gestured toward the car court. "Pilar suggested we run away right then. My car was parked down there. I thought she was joking. But she slid behind the wheel—she barely fit with her huge belly—and turned the key I had left in the ignition. Before I knew what was happening, the car lurched forward. I jumped into the car and tried to stop her. Flavio wasn't fast enough."

Maya squeezed her eyes against the memory. "Pilar didn't know how to drive, so when she stomped on the gas pedal, the car shot out onto the street like a bullet. She was happy and laughing, and the wind was slapping her long hair across her face. I pleaded with her to stop, but a split second later, she swerved to avoid hitting someone. She lost control of the car and it slammed against that rock at the edge of the beach. The car flipped…I don't know how many times. I was thrown free, but she was trapped behind the wheel." Maya gulped back a sob. "It all happened so quickly," she whispered.

"But I always thought you were driving," Carlotta said, clutching her hand.

With shaking hands, Maya reached for a glass of water from the nightstand and gulped it down. Tears rimmed her eyes, and she brought her sister's hand to her heart. "That's what I told our parents. For me to let Pilar drive would have been beyond reckless—it would have been unconscionable. She'd never been behind the wheel, but Pilar thought if I could drive, she could, too. I don't think our parents believed me, but I felt so guilty that I had to claim the responsibility."

Ivy slid her fingers along the old piece of paper she'd tucked into her pocket. She hardly dared ask the question, but she had to. "And the baby?"

Tears slipped down Maya's cheeks. "By the time I awoke in the hospital, Pilar and the baby were both gone. We never knew if our dear sister carried a girl or a boy. The nuns who staffed the hospital told us it had been impossible to tell after the accident. The thought of that was so sad."

"I think I can answer that." Ivy brought out the paper. "I found this tucked in back of the sketch." She read the date, and Maya nodded. Then she read the rest. "It says, *baby girl*."

Maya gasped. "They knew and didn't tell us?" She embraced Carlotta, sobbing against her shoulder.

Ivy rested her hand on her aunt's narrow back. "Perhaps they only meant to ease your grief." Maybe the nuns thought if the baby did not have an identity, the loss would be less painful over time.

Learning this story and watching her mother and her aunt —even now, still grieving for their sister—Ivy blinked back tears of her own.

Maya clung to Carlotta. "If only I hadn't left my keys in the car or if I'd tried harder to stop her. I was utterly devastated—it was the end of my life as I'd known it. I couldn't face you or our parents without thinking about the pain I'd inflicted on all of you."

"It was simply a tragic accident," Carlotta said. "That's what I was told."

"But there was so much more." Maya shook her head. "The tighter I held this secret, the worse it became. I couldn't bear to talk about it or face any of you. If I never saw you, I could pretend none of it had happened, but it gnawed at me every day until my insides were raw. I prayed so hard for forgiveness, yet I never felt deserving of it. In the end, I robbed you, my dear Carlotta, of both your sisters. And my children hardly knew their grandparents or the rest of the family."

Maya's deep sobs were heartbreaking, but Carlotta embraced her sister and waited until her grief was spent. Ivy sat beside her aunt with her hand on her shoulder, offering her the support she needed until, at last, Maya was quiet.

"You've suffered enough," Carlotta said, gazing into her sister's eyes. "If you're ready, I would love to have you back in my life. Let's not waste the time we have left."

"I'd like that," Maya said, sniffing. "I've missed you so much, but I worried that you'd think I was a horrible person if you knew what I'd done."

Carlotta smoothed wisps of hair from her sister's face. "I might have been the youngest, but I remember how impetuous Pilar was. Had I been in your place, I'm sure I couldn't have reined her in either."

Ivy eased from the edge of the bed. "I'm looking forward to spending a lot more time with you, Aunt Maya." She smiled and added, "Tia Maya."

Maya held out her hands and beamed at Ivy. "I always thought your mother was bragging about you, but now I see she was entirely justified."

Ivy embraced her, grateful for the chance to be reunited. Maya was a woman she wanted to know better now.

Ivy excused herself and left them alone to catch up on the time they had lost. Her mother had been determined to reunite with Maya, but neither of them had suspected the secret she had harbored for so many years.

Ivy made her way downstairs. She could hear Shelly tending to Daisy with Poppy and Sunny in the kitchen. Wanting to see Pilar's sketch with fresh eyes, Ivy made her way to her art studio at the rear of the house.

She slid onto a stool and gazed at Pilar's expressive eyes. This time, in the young woman's shy gaze, she saw courage and hope. Knowing the story behind this sketch and the love Pilar had for Flavio and their unborn child gave Ivy a deeper appreciation.

She touched the edge of the thick paper. Finding Pilar's portrait had been a stroke of luck, and in a sense, served history. Learning that the child Pilar had carried was a little girl meant a lot to Maya and Carlotta.

"Thank you for keeping this secret safe," she said softly. Amelia Erickson's actions might have become odd as her illness grew, but what she treasured, she kept as safe as her mind could grasp.

Ivy wondered how life might have worked out for Pilar and Flavio if they had been allowed to follow their hearts and marry. That had been a time of forged alliances and arranged marriages in certain families—and it hadn't been that long ago. Young women—hardly more than girls—might have been viewed as mere chattel to bind families and merge businesses. Ivy sighed at the thought, which she knew was not entirely outdated.

She arranged the portrait on an easel and stepped back to admire it. The only thing left to do was to share her aunt's story with her sisters and others. Honey and Shelly, and Poppy, Sunny, and Misty. Pilar's heart-wrenching life was part of their history, and they all deserved to know how she had lived and died.

Ivy opened the door and paused. Happy laughter echoed through the house now. Her mother and sister had been reunited, and her aunt had unburdened herself. Ivy didn't want to put a damper on the festivities. Surely this sad story could wait a little longer. What difference could it possibly make? She shut the door to her studio.

15

*I*vy woke to the sound of birds and the smell of coffee. That meant that Bennett was in the kitchen, and a cup of coffee would soon appear on her nightstand. He might indulge her, but she also enjoyed returning the favors. She cuddled her pillow, enjoying the extra minutes until he joined her. They had slept later this morning than usual.

After a poolside barbecue that Mitch had managed, intent on making a good impression, which he did—score one for him—and a long night of laughter around the firepit, Ivy had fallen into bed feeling pleased that the reunion was off to a good start.

Bennett padded across the wooden floor wearing a white cotton robe she'd bought for him tied loosely around his trim hips. In his hands, he held their morning coffee in their favorite earthenware mugs.

His gaze roved over her, despite the fact that Ivy's hair was undoubtedly a mess, and she probably had pillow creases on her cheeks. It felt good to be admired after so many years of being picked apart for imperfections. She stretched luxuriously under the covers.

Bennett kissed her softly. "Good morning, gorgeous."

His voice was slightly hoarse from singing on the beach late last night as he strummed his guitar, much to the delight of their relatives—a point for Bennett, too. "Would you like your coffee here or in the treehouse?" he asked.

The sun was already streaming through the windows—a good omen for the day ahead.

"Let's sit outside."

She shrugged into a matching terrycloth robe and followed him onto their new balcony overlooking the ocean through the palm trees. After taking her coffee from him, she tucked her feet under her legs on the outdoor sofa, enjoying the morning breeze off the water. She ignored the finishes and painting still needed. They'd get around to that.

Suspended above the beach, the outdoor balcony was a cozy escape. To her, this was paradise.

More than that, she realized paradise didn't mean perfection.

Bennet sat beside her. "That was a fascinating story Maya shared last night. This old house harbors a lot of history."

Ivy shook her head, still amazed at her aunt's revelation. "It's amazing to think my family had a close connection to this place. And that my grandmother Isabella knew Amelia."

"It's not that surprising, though. The coastal communities were smaller then. Families who had been here a long time often knew each other. Especially if they moved in certain social circles, as your grandparents and the Ericksons seemed to."

"I suppose so," Ivy said. Still, she couldn't help thinking there might be more to the story.

Bennett put his arm around her shoulder. "Your family's Spanish land grant history is interesting. I'd like to hear how it came about."

Ivy grew thoughtful. "Mom and Aunt Maya could tell you more about that, although, in retrospect, it wasn't really fair to the indigenous population. My grandparents recognized that, and as they sold land, they made some bequests to descendants in the area for schools, housing, and infrastructure. I didn't even know about that until just a few years ago."

"Families often have a lot of forgotten history."

"Not much anymore now that everything is online. Maybe that's why I was so surprised at my aunt's revelation." Last night, Ivy had told Bennett more of the details that her aunt had shared. Although the younger generation, including Misty and Sunny, had listened in rapt attention around the firepit, Maya had grown weary and skipped parts of the story she'd shared with Carlotta and Ivy. She wished her father had been able to get a flight to share the evening. It was a shame that he was missing this, but at least he would be here soon.

Bennett took her hand and squeezed it.

Just having him close made Ivy feel as if all was right in her world. In hindsight, she recognized how seldom she'd felt that with her first husband. Every marriage was different, she realized. Struck by that feeling, she sipped her coffee and smiled at Bennett over the rim. "Have I told you how much I love you today?"

He drew her closer. "Even if you didn't, I'd know."

They chatted a little more about the day ahead, and Ivy glanced around their open-air enclave hidden among the palms. The old and new sections of the structure flowed well. "Sometimes I wonder if we'll ever learn all of this old home's secrets?"

"I hope we'll have plenty of time to find out." Bennett gulped the last of his coffee and stood. "It's early, but I need a quick run before breakfast and the beach Olympics begin."

"I haven't heard anyone stirring yet. I'd better assist with the breakfast buffet."

"Need some help?"

"No, but I appreciate it. Poppy shamed Reed and Rocky into taking this morning's shift. Go get your run in before the day gets away from you."

"Want to join me? I'll walk some with you."

Ivy threaded her arms around her husband. "Judging from the activities Poppy and the others have scheduled, I think I'll get plenty of exercise today."

Bennett laughed. "Relay races and volleyball today, right?"

"And a lot more."

He paused to kiss her again. "I'll be there. But I do have some business to tend to when I return."

"A real estate client?" She tried to hide her disappointment. This weekend was for family.

"You know how they can be," Bennett said quickly. "I won't be long, I promise." He disappeared into the bedroom, and when he emerged, he wore his running gear. With another quick kiss, he was off.

Although she was a little disappointed, Bennett generally juggled his commitments well. She blew out a breath and adjusted her attitude. If he said he wouldn't be long, she could count on that.

Ivy listened to his steps on the staircase outside. All things considered, this was indeed her slice of paradise.

Just then, she heard her phone buzz. She checked, saw that it was Shelly, and answered. "You're up early."

"Daisy woke me. At least she waited until daybreak this time." Shelly hesitated. "There's something I need to talk to you about before everyone gathers."

"Come help me put out breakfast. Mitch should be dropping off muffins soon. Reed and Rocky are on the schedule to help, but I wouldn't be surprised if they overslept."

"I'll pick up the muffins and be right there."

Ivy drained her coffee and dressed, thinking about what Shelly wanted to talk about and all the cousins that were gathering at the house today. Flint and Forrest had a slew of children—nine between them—and they were awfully competitive. Ivy had already warned Darla that there might be a lot of noise. Mitch had invited her to the barbecue last night, and Darla had been pleased to meet everyone, as if they were her new adopted family.

Their long-term resident, Gilda, had decided to take Pixie for a visit to a friend's home, where the Chihuahua would be more comfortable. With the heightened activity in the house, that was a wise decision. Ivy was happy to adjust her monthly bill, even though Gilda didn't ask for it.

Without any outside guests, this was one of the few days of the year that the Seabreeze Inn was simply a family home, just as it had once been. Ivy wondered how many other family dinners and reunions had taken place here over the years. Surely Amelia—if she still existed, in whatever form—would be happy about this gathering.

Ivy paused her hairbrush in hand, staring behind her in the mirror as if Amelia might be lurking.

She had just zipped up a bright floral summer shift when she heard Shelly's footsteps on the stairs. "It's open; come in."

Shelly stepped inside. "I had no idea how much exercise I'd be getting toting Daisy around." She bounced the little one on her hip. "If I'm not buff by the end of the year, I'm going to file a complaint." She pushed her sunglasses over her hair. "Hey, hot colors. I like that on you."

"Thanks. Another vintage steal." She slipped on the embellished white sneakers she'd splurged on with what she'd saved. "Come with me. We can set up breakfast while we talk."

"Can't it wait?"

"People will be up soon."

Shelly frowned. "Can't all those giant kids manage on their own?"

Ivy remembered her mother's advice about Shelly. Her sister appeared to be regaining her energy, and Ivy thought she might be feeling better. Still, after considering how estranged their mother and Maya had become, Ivy shifted her priorities. If Shelly needed her now, everything could wait.

She gestured toward the sofa. "I'm sure they can manage. What's up?"

Shelly perched on a cushion and eased Daisy beside her. "I was thinking about our conversation last night. I'm still shocked that our grandmother and Amelia knew each other. A thousand questions have been swirling in my head, like how they met, and how close they might have been."

Sitting with her sister, Ivy nodded thoughtfully. "I suppose they were close enough for Isabella to entrust Pilar to her care."

"It's pretty cool to know Amelia took in one of our kin a long time ago."

Daisy kicked off a sock, and Ivy stretched it back onto her tiny foot. "Considering the social mores of the time, Summer Beach was just far enough from the family home for Pilar to hide her pregnancy here, but close enough that Isabella could visit her daughter."

Shelly grimaced at that. "I couldn't imagine if I'd been pregnant and hidden away like that. Times have really changed, haven't they?"

"In a lot of places. In others, not so much." Ivy wondered what was on Shelly's mind, but her sister seemed to be talking around whatever it was.

Shelly nodded. "Pilar was probably scared to tell her parents."

"Most likely."

"Being sent away, even for a short distance, had to have been traumatic. But then Flavio came back for her." Shelly's expression lifted at the thought. "Imagine how romantic that was."

Ivy nodded. "I think Mom feels a lot better knowing that Pilar and Flavio became engaged shortly before she died."

Shelly's eyes were bright in the morning light. "Do you think Flavio went back to Spain?"

"Aunt Maya said he did. He must have been broken-hearted over the twin losses of Pilar and their child."

"I wonder if he's still alive."

"He might be."

"Maybe we could find him."

Ivy raised her brow. "You're taking a sudden interest in our family tree."

"Since Mitch and I did our DNA tests, I've been thinking about family a lot more. Maybe Flavio would like to know that his baby was a girl."

Ivy drew in her lower lip. "That was a long time ago, Shells."

"Mom and Maya seemed relieved to know."

"But that was their sister."

"He loved her, too. That was his child she carried."

Ivy was doubtful, yet Shelly had a point. "I understand, but remember…Flavio is now an older man from a traditional family in Spain. Would he want to be reminded of something that happened in the wilds of California so long ago? He might have a wife and children who know nothing of his past. Flavio might not welcome this new detail. Worse, it could stir up a lot of trouble for him."

"But it's the truth, Ives." Although her voice wavered, Shelly was sticking to her point. "Doesn't everyone want to know the truth?"

Ivy wasn't so sure of that. "Maybe not always. You should talk to Mom. If you really want to contact Flavio, Aunt Maya would be the one to make the introduction or deliver the news. She knew him. That's the proper way to go about it."

Shelly brushed back wisps of hair with irritation. "Sounds antiquated to me."

Just then, Daisy began to kick her legs and wave her arms. A small cry escaped her lips, and Shelly checked her. "Time for another change, and I left her diapers in the house."

"And I need to check on breakfast."

"You have a head start. I left the muffins in the kitchen."

Ivy paused, not meaning to pry but wanting to support Shelly. She touched her sister's hand. "Besides all that, how are you feeling?"

Smiling shyly, Shelly grasped her hand. "Better, thanks. It helps to know I'm not alone. And that feeling overwhelmed is totally normal. Somehow, that makes it more manageable."

"Are you sure you're up for a wild weekend? You can slip away to rest whenever you want. Mom and I can look after Daisy."

"I'll let you know, but I'm really looking forward to seeing everyone. And Mitch is feeling less apprehensive, too."

"Everyone loved his burgers and barbecue."

Shelly grinned. "They did, didn't they?"

As they walked downstairs, Ivy thought about Shelly's questions. Her sister was becoming more aware of their family, and her place in it, which Ivy supposed was natural after having a child.

Ivy paused at the bottom of the stairway. "Have you found out much about Mitch's family through the DNA analysis?"

"Some. He's making some calls. So far, no health issues of any real concern have surfaced."

"That's good. And we're a fairly healthy lot. You must feel better knowing that now."

"It's what we wanted." Her sister glanced toward the kitchen, which was suddenly bustling with activity.

Shelly patted Daisy's back as they crossed the car court. "I still need some advice, though."

Before Ivy could reply, Sunny bounded from the kitchen. "The guys let us down, so Misty and I will make breakfast for everyone."

Shelly twisted her lips to one side. "This is a big, hungry crowd. You'll need help."

"We'll pitch in." Sensing Shelly's disappointment, Ivy put her arm around her sister. "I promise we'll talk later."

16

*I*n the kitchen, Ivy's oldest daughter stood at the vintage stove, adjusting the flame under a large skillet while Poppy cracked eggs into a bowl.

Poppy turned around. "Guess you heard that Reed and Rocky are still recovering after whatever they did last night. My brothers can be so irresponsible—they drive me nuts."

"Beer on the beach is what I heard," Sunny said. She pulled out a skillet and opened a package of bacon.

Ivy grinned. "I'm sure you and your sisters will even the score." Poppy's sisters, Summer and Coral, had arrived last night, too.

"You bet we will." Misty stirred the thickening eggs over a burner. "As for breakfast, scrambled eggs are fast and easy. You must have six dozen eggs in that little refrigerator."

"That's because we have a lot of mouths to feed—and an egg-and-spoon race." Ivy watched Sunny, who was fastidiously arranging bacon in another large skillet. "I have a shortcut for you. With a crowd this size, we should put the bacon in the oven. Reed and Rocky could polish off all that in two minutes."

Poppy smirked. "When they get their lazy you-know-whats out of bed. Dad will take care of them."

"Isn't that cheating?" Sunny asked. "Cooking bacon like that, I mean."

"People here are hardly bacon connoisseurs," Ivy said. "Unless you want to stand over a hot skillet half the morning, this is much easier. And we'll need more than one package of bacon." She plucked an apron from a hook. "Poppy, would you bring out the rest of the bacon in Gertie? I'll need to shop for more today."

Poppy reached into one of the twin vintage turquoise refrigerators. "We're going to the grocery store and farmers market later today. Just tell us what you need."

"And I'm off to change Daisy," Shelly said, pushing through the kitchen door.

"Let's finish our talk later," Ivy called after her. She sensed Shelly had more to say, but she could hear footsteps upstairs and on the stairs. They had hungry guests to feed. Flint and Forrest would be arriving soon, and their families with them.

"How is the activity schedule coming along?" Ivy asked as she showed Sunny how to arrange the bacon on baking sheets.

"It's all done, and it's going to be a lot of fun, Mom." Misty stirred the scrambled eggs as she spoke. "Poppy made the list. She's more like you than Sunny or me."

Ivy kissed her eldest daughter's cheek. "You inherited my artistic bent."

"Here it is." Poppy showed her a printed schedule. "We'll start with some icebreakers over breakfast. We'll warm up with a tug-o-war rope competition and a relay race. Then we'll have a hula hoop contest to rest a little, followed by an egg-and-spoon race."

"I'm looking forward to the tacky tourist party tonight," Misty added, sounding excited. "We'll give out awards for best costumes and the farthest traveled. And we're coordinating with Mitch on the luau theme for our beach cookout."

"That will be a lot of fun," Poppy said. "Imani will provide floral leis, and people will wear sarongs and Hawaiian shirts. Sunny will lead a shopping expedition in the village for those that don't have them. For dinner, we'll grill lots of pineapple, pork, and seafood, serve fruity drinks, and play Hawaiian music. Leilani and Roy are helping us compile the playlist and the menu."

Ivy was impressed by their plans. Poppy and Sunny had assured her they would handle the activities, so she had entrusted that to them while she oversaw the accommodations with Shelly. "Beth is shooting video for Shelly, but we'll have lots of photos, right?"

Sunny grinned. "Elena and I plan to create bound and printed photo books as a surprise after the event. They'll be really nice, Mom."

"I'm sure they will be. Your grandparents will be delighted with everything you've planned."

"We wanted to make it extra special for them," Misty said.

"I'm so proud of you all." Despite the breakfast slip-up, everything was running as planned. Ivy was looking forward to a wonderful reunion with cousins she hadn't seen in years.

Sunny opened the oven and slid in the baking sheets. "There, that's done. Thanks for sharing your shortcut, Mom."

Ivy watched the young women, who were all quite competent in the kitchen. This was the next generation, she thought with satisfaction. The Bay and Reina families were in good hands. She imagined everything would run smoothly at the reunion.

Ivy was especially glad to see Sunny joining in the effort with her sister and cousins. As the youngest, she'd often felt left out, which might have explained her early behavioral issues. Ivy hoped Sunny had passed that phase.

"If you have breakfast under control, I need to check on Shelly."

"Sure, Mom," Misty said. "See you later."

Ivy made her way toward the downstairs powder room where Shelly was changing Daisy. They had added a changing table, which guests appreciated, too. Just before she entered, a younger woman opened the front door and stepped inside.

"Hello," Ivy said, crossing to the foyer. "Welcome to the Seabreeze Inn. Are you here to see a guest?"

"Not exactly," the woman replied.

"I'm afraid we're full. We're having a family reunion, so the inn is closed to outsiders."

The woman's dark green eyes widened. "A reunion?"

"That's right. But I hope you'll return. And I'm happy to recommend the Seal Cove Inn nearby."

"I'm not here for a room." The woman's face was flushed pink against soft brown hair that fell loosely around her shoulders.

Early to mid-thirties, Ivy guessed, and neatly dressed as if she were meeting someone special or going to brunch. "How might I help you, then?"

"Is Shelly Bay Kline here?"

"Yes, but she's tending to her baby right now. I'm her sister, Ivy. Maybe I can help you."

"Her sister?"

"That's right." The younger woman seemed nervous.

The woman looked around as if making sure they were alone. "I know this is going to sound outlandish, but I'm registered on an ancestry site. I had my DNA analyzed, and it looks like I'm related to Shelly Bay Kline. And to you, too, I guess. I'm June."

Ivy stared at her. This is what she'd been worried about. "I'm sorry, this isn't a good time." She paused. "Are you sure about this?"

"I'm pretty certain, unless the DNA was wrong." June gave her a hopeful smile.

"Oh, I see." She drew a steadying breath. "Was Shelly expecting you?"

"No, but we emailed," June replied, her voice wavering slightly. "I was nearby, so I thought I'd see if she was in."

Ivy's mind whirred like a pinball machine, with wild thoughts pinging around her head. "Won't you have a seat? I'll get Shelly for you. And we'll figure this out, won't we?" She gestured toward the parlor.

"I hope so, thanks." June took a seat.

Any minute, the rest of the family would be arriving for a late breakfast. Ivy hurried toward the powder room and burst in. "Shelly, that woman's name is June, isn't it?"

Her sister looked up, her eyes wide with shock. "I can explain, but keep your voice down. Daisy is just drifting off. Did she contact you?"

"She's here." Ivy lowered her voice to a hoarse whisper. "She says she's related to us through your DNA sample. She wants to meet you."

"Now?"

"Well, of course, *now*. Right when the entire family is gathering." Ivy pressed a hand to her forehead.

"I was still hoping it might be a mistake."

"Evidently not. Did you invite her here?"

"No, but..."

"But what?"

"Beth might have. She did some more investigating."

Ivy felt her blood pressure rising. "Did she find out how this woman is related to us?"

Daisy stirred in Shelly's arms. "I'm not sure. And keep your voice down."

"This is a disaster, and you want me to be quiet? Shelly, you have to fix this before everyone arrives." Ivy drew her hands over her face. "I can't believe this is happening. Who did she trace to? Was it Mom or Dad? Or our grandparents? Or someone else?"

"I'm not sure how to read all those percentages. This is what I wanted to ask you about this morning."

"I wish you had so we could have stopped her from coming. Oh, Shelly, how could you let this happen in the middle of our reunion?"

"Shhh. Daisy is trying to sleep," Shelly whispered.

"And I'm trying to avoid a disaster. Why didn't you tell me about she was planning to land on our doorstep?"

"Because I didn't know. There isn't exactly a right time for it, you know." Daisy squirmed and let out a cry. "Now she's awake," Shelly said with an accusing glare.

"Well, I guess June will get to meet her, too." Ivy desperately tried to think of a solution. "Is Beth planning on filming this morning?"

Shelly groaned. "I'll try to stop her."

"This is no one else's business but our own," Ivy said. "Let's face this and figure it out together. Like adults."

Daisy wailed at that, and Shelly bounced her in her lap.

Ivy twisted her lips to one side. "I feel like that, too, kiddo." Carlotta's words floated to mind. *Stay calm, be nice*, she recalled, repeating the words to herself like a mantra. "Let's ask her to come in here."

"In the bathroom?"

Ivy threw up her hands. "Where would you suggest we talk to find out who in our family has been concealing a secret baby? Judging by her age, it's an old secret, too." Ivy swallowed, trying to get a grip on her nerves. Suddenly, another thought occurred to her. "Unless there has been an error. That happens all the time, I'm sure. Right?"

Shelly cast a glum look her way.

On the other side of the door, footsteps pounded across the floor, and the house erupted with the noise of a boisterous family. The cousins were racing downstairs for breakfast.

And now, there is one more of us, Ivy thought. "I've got it. Let's take her to my place."

"Is Bennett there?"

"He went for a quick run, but he also has to meet a client."

Shelly twisted her lips to one side. "If he's there, at least he can be impartial."

"Look, I'm trying to clean up your mess here."

"*My* mess?" Shelly glared at her. "Don't pin this on me. It's whoever was doing the hanky-panky way back when—it's their mess. I just can't believe that Mom or Dad would have—"

Ivy cut her off with a glare. Pacing the small anteroom, she pressed a hand to her pounding heart. "Until five minutes ago, the reunion was off to a fabulous start. I know it's not your fault, but the timing couldn't be worse for us to discover a half-sister. Or whatever she purports to be."

Shelly looked up from beneath damp lashes. "Do you think it might have been Dad?"

"I can't imagine that." Ivy swallowed against a lump in her throat. "Mom?"

"She'd never give up a child. Maybe Honey?"

"I don't think so. I would've remembered."

"Well, it's not us." Shelly inclined her head. "Wait. How old did you say she is?"

"We don't have time to do the math. June is waiting in the parlor, and we need to get her out of there before someone gets chatty with her."

Shelly rose, patting Daisy on the back to calm her cries. "Okay. Let's do this."

Moving with leaden feet, Ivy opened the door and started for the foyer. Yet, for all the despair she felt, she could only imagine what June was feeling. Assuming the younger woman wasn't a fortune seeker—she could have set her sights higher if she were—Ivy had to admire June's courage to step into a den of Bays on their turf.

As with Aunt Maya, maybe the situation wasn't what it

seemed. Changing her perception about her aunt had taken an intervention from her mother.

If June was right—but no, how could she be? Surely there had been a mistake, Ivy thought, grasping at an alternate explanation. They'd sort this out and go back to the reunion schedule.

Unless the DNA was correct. And it usually was.

Ivy whispered, "Do you recall how much courage it took for you and Mitch to send in your DNA test?"

"We agonized over it for a few weeks."

"Multiply that feeling by a thousand. June could have called, but she's here, facing what she thinks needs to be done."

Shelly looked thoughtful. "Sounds a lot like a Bay family trait."

"Maybe she's one of us after all." Adjusting her attitude—which wasn't as easy as it sounded—Ivy resolved to make June as comfortable as she could while they figured this out. Maybe it was all just a silly mistake that they'd have a good laugh about.

Or not.

But as they approached the younger woman, Ivy's heart lurched. Her nephew Rocky had arrived and was talking to June. And Beth was walking toward them.

Ivy tugged on Shelly's arm. "I'll take June," she whispered. "And you can handle Beth. We can't let them talk. Now, go."

"I'll meet you at your place," Shelly said, quickening her step.

17

*B*ennett didn't like misleading Ivy. There was no client he needed to meet with—that had been an outright lie. Still, it was for a good cause, he'd told himself.

He drummed his fingers on the steering wheel of his SUV, watching travelers who'd been on overnight flights streaming from the baggage terminal.

An officer signaled for him to move on to keep the traffic flowing.

Bennett sighed. He'd been circling the airport for an hour. San Diego was quite a change from the quiet town of Summer Beach.

Once again, Bennett put his vehicle in gear to leave, but just before he pulled from the curb, a tall, trim man with thick silver hair and a backpack emerged from the airport. Ivy's father had been on a long flight from Sydney, Australia. Quickly, Bennett waved, and the officer nodded for him to remain.

Sterling Bay hurried toward him. "Good to see you, son. Thanks for the lift to the inn."

"My pleasure." Bennett hugged his father-in-law. Despite the distance, they'd kept in touch via emails and calls when

Sterling was in port. They both enjoyed boating, and Sterling had been a distance runner in his youth. Bennett eyed the backpack. Sterling was traveling light. "Any other bags?"

"I'll need help with two big bags behind me." Sterling grinned and turned toward the baggage terminal.

Just then, Ivy's older sister and her husband, an active-looking couple, appeared in the sliding glass doorway. Bennett hadn't expected them to come as well, but he was awfully pleased they had. And the family would be thrilled. "Well, would you look at this. I thought Honey and Gabe were taking the boat out while you were gone."

"That was merely a diversionary tactic." Sterling chuckled. "We wanted it to be a surprise."

"Elena knows," Honey said. "How could I not tell our daughter?" She greeted Bennett with a hug. "It's so good to see you again, although it's been too long."

Gabe gave him a hearty hug as well. "Our Ivy has done well with the likes of you."

"I'm the lucky one."

"That makes two of us, mate."

Bennett put their backpacks and luggage in the back of the SUV. For having been on such a long and connecting flight from Sydney, they were in remarkably good spirits. After months at sea, Sterling looked even more fit. His silver hair looked brighter against his suntanned face. "Looks like sailing is agreeing with you."

"It's been a real dream for us."

Gabe leaned in. "I even got him up on a surfboard on Bondi Beach before we left."

Honey wagged a finger at her husband. "And nearly missed the flight."

"We're here, aren't we?" Gabe grinned and hugged his wife.

Bennett hoped he and Ivy would still be as happy as her parents and Gabe and Honey were after all their years of marriage. He suspected the lives they'd chosen had a lot to do with it. When a person enjoyed what they did, life had more meaning. Gabe ran a concession with surfboards and other beach gear near the famous Bondi Beach, and Honey owned a boutique nearby. Gabe had a health scare a few years back, so he and Honey had worked together to adjust his diet and lifestyle. He was certainly the picture of health now.

Bennett activated the ignition and eased the vehicle from the airport terminal. "Next stop, Summer Beach." He imagined Ivy's surprise when they arrived. That would be well worth his little fib.

When they reached the inn, Elena was waiting eagerly by the door. "Mom, Dad!" She flew into their arms.

"My goodness, you're looking so thin," Honey said, ruffling Elena's short dark hair.

"Oh, Mom." Elena smiled at her mother.

Gabe chuckled. "She's perfect, aren't you, snugglepot? Your mother just wants to cook for you."

"Now, don't call her that," Honey said, feigning indignation. "Our Elena is all grown up and making a name for herself in Hollywood."

"Wait until you see what we have planned," Elena said, taking her mother's hand. "Let's go surprise everyone. They're all inside having breakfast—courtesy of yours truly, along with Misty, Sunny, and Poppy. Since there are so many of us, we're all helping out in the kitchen. You're going to eat well this week. Mitch and Bennett are planning to barbecue for the luau."

"I can help on the barbie," Gabe said. "Even brought my special spice rub for you."

Just then, Carlotta flew from the kitchen door. "*Mi amor!*"

Sterling swept his wife into his arms. "My darling, how I've missed you." They'd been apart these months since Shelly had given birth. "How are Shelly and Daisy?"

"Waiting for you." Carlotta looked around. "Somewhere. They were just here a few minutes ago."

"I saw them going upstairs to your place with Ivy," Elena said. "They were with a friend."

"Or a relative we haven't met yet," Sterling said, chuckling. "Too many Bays on this shore, am I right? Won't be long before the grandkids start families."

"Reed has a serious girlfriend," Elena said. "She's really nice, so we're trying not to overwhelm her and scare her away."

Bennett could understand that. He hoped they wouldn't be too hard on Mitch, although he already knew the family from Southern California. It was the East Coast family that neither of them had met before.

"I'll go upstairs and get Ivy and Shelly," Bennett said.

Honey pressed a finger to her lips. "Don't tell them Gabe and I are here."

"I'll let that be a surprise."

"I can hardly wait to see little Daisy," Sterling said. "Maybe I should have come earlier."

"You're here now, *mi corazón*," Carlotta said, drawing a hand over her husband's shoulder. "You had to tend to the boat repairs and spend time with Honey and Gabe. I understand. We have to spread ourselves around these days."

While the group went inside to surprise the rest of the relatives, Bennett started upstairs. He wondered who was visiting Ivy, not that their house wasn't open to everyone. As he climbed the stairs, he could hear murmured voices. Ivy, Shelly, and someone else. They sounded serious. Was Daisy alright? He hoped everything was okay, especially this close to the festivities they'd planned.

He opened the door, and the three women turned to him. Ivy, Shelly, and another woman who shared some of the same features. She had to be another relative.

"Welcome, I'm Bennett, Ivy's husband." He approached

the group, ready to share the good news. Despite the happy occasion, he detected a cloud of tension in the room. He darted a look at Ivy, whose lips were pressed together as if she were holding something back. Turning to the new woman, he asked, "Did you just arrive from the East Coast?"

Instead of answering, the woman looked shyly between Ivy and Shelly, who was cradling Daisy. The baby was quiet but wide awake as if she was entranced by the new person in the room.

"This is June," Ivy said evenly. "Bennett is also the mayor of Summer Beach."

"Hello, June. I'm assuming you're part of this wild family. Welcome, we have a lot of festivities and good food planned. Have you met the rest of the Summer Beach family?"

"About that," Ivy said, looking flushed.

"June came to see me," Shelly said quickly.

Their visitor looked up. "It's nice to meet you. But I won't be staying. I didn't mean to be any trouble. I didn't realize you were having a reunion. If I had, I wouldn't have bothered you."

"Please, stay," Bennett said. "There's plenty to go around. And we have a surprise inside." From the corner of his eye, he saw Ivy give an almost imperceptible shake of her head.

"We have one here, too," Shelly said, her eyes widening.

What was going on? All three women looked awkward and agitated. "Would someone like to fill me in?"

Ivy held her hand out to him. "Please sit down."

Bennett eased next to his wife, but he didn't want to keep the party inside waiting. "Ivy, Shelly, I came to tell you that your father has arrived. I picked him up at the airport this morning. He wanted to surprise everyone."

"I thought you had a client meeting," Ivy said. Her eyes lit, and Shelly smiled. "We'll be right there." Turning to June, Ivy added, "Our father has just arrived from Sydney for the reunion. We haven't seen him in months, and he hasn't seen Daisy yet."

"I understand," June said quickly, rising.

Ivy touched June's hand. "But before you go, let's ask Bennett for his opinion." With what Bennett recognized as forced calm, Ivy began. "Shelly and Mitch had their DNA analyzed so they could examine their family health history for Daisy's benefit. She's fine, but there was another surprise."

Shelly looked up. "It seems that June and I—Ivy, too, I imagine—are somehow related."

Bennett took a moment to process this. He drew a hand over his chin, considering the options.

June's face flushed, and she stood up. "I shouldn't have come."

"No, we're glad you did," Ivy said. "It's just that it's a surprise."

Bennett laced his hands and leaned forward toward June. "Do you have a birth certificate or other documents that might explain how you're related?"

"I can bring a copy of my mother's birth certificate, but it doesn't mean much. Her mother told her she was adopted when she was a teenager, but her birth certificate was amended, so she doesn't know who her biological parents are."

"Does she want to know?" Bennett asked.

June hesitated, seeming to choose her words with care. "She did at one time, but she told me that she was happy with her parents, and she was afraid that if she found out who her birth parents were, it might bring up a lot of unpleasant history. My grandparents were wonderful people. He was a surgeon, and she was a nurse. My grandmother would only say that it was a private adoption. I'm not sure what that means, other than the records were closed. If they even existed. Back then, things were done differently."

Ivy held up her hands. "I don't know what to do. If the

DNA is correct, then someone in the family is concealing a secret. We want to acknowledge June, but we're not sure what the connection is or who to talk to about this."

Shelly cleared her throat. "I ordered the DNA through Beth. Her staff can help us figure this out. That's what they do."

"You have a point," Bennett said. "Of course, that would mean outing someone. Is Beth planning to make this an episode on her show?"

The three women traded looks.

"My mother and I wouldn't want that," June said softly. "I understand this is awkward for you."

Bennett tried again. Turning to June, he asked, "Is there anything else you have that might be helpful?"

June began to shake her head, then she paused and seemed to recall something. "My grandmother saved a few mementos. My mom didn't know if they were real or something her mother created to make her feel like her birth mother really loved her. I know that sounds strange, but my grandmother loved to make up stories."

Shelly nodded. "I think people did that back then. Without the internet or social media, they could recreate entire histories. Old movie stars often did that and usually got away with it. Until now."

"That's exactly what I suspected," June said. "This all seems so complicated, but I would really like to know. See, it's just my mom and me now. I've always thought if I could find some of her kin, she wouldn't feel so lonely. My father passed away when I was young, and she never remarried."

Ivy reached for June's hand. "I'm sorry about your father. My daughters lost their dad, so I understand." With a quick look at Bennett, she added, "Could you come back tomorrow? We'll figure out what to do, but if you could bring those items, maybe someone in the family will recognize them. It might help you find some answers."

"For all of us," Shelly added.

June dabbed her eyes. "I can do that. Tomorrow will be a special day. I knew this would be difficult, and I appreciate your being so understanding."

"I'll walk you out," Bennett said. "I know Ivy and Shelly are eager to see their father."

They all agreed on a time to meet the next day before Ivy and Shelly left. Bennett walked June out.

The younger woman paused by her car. "Thanks for listening in there. I know this is unexpected and that Ivy and Shelly are doing their best."

"Those two have a way of figuring out the nearly impossible. And for the record, you couldn't find a nicer family." He chuckled, thinking about the festivities they had planned. "Maybe a little competitive, but they like to have fun."

June gave him a quick smile and tucked her hair behind her ear. The small motion reminded Bennett of Ivy. June's eyes were nearly the same shade as Ivy's unusual, deep green eyes. Two percent of the population, he recalled, thinking about the statistics he'd read about green eyes. That narrowed the odds quite a bit. He held the car door for June and then watched her drive away.

Bennett could see the family resemblance in her, even if Ivy and Shelly couldn't. The question was, who in the family had given up a child? Or who—what man, that is—might have had a child they didn't know existed? Bennett thought he knew the Bay family well, but this situation revealed that even the best among them might still harbor secrets.

18

*A*fter breakfast, everyone spilled onto the patio in the sunshine of a beautiful, cloudless morning. They were all dressed in colorful beach gear—shorts, tank tops, and a few bathing suits with cover-ups. With her white shorts, Ivy wore one of the bright yellow T-shirts Poppy had made. It read *Bay and Reina Reunion, Summer Beach.* Other family members donned them as well.

They all gathered for a group photo. Beth volunteered to take the photo, and she was also prepared to video.

After taking the photo, Beth turned to Ivy and Shelly. "Who did you say that woman was who came in?"

"I didn't," Shelly replied.

"A friend," Ivy quickly said.

"Oh. I thought she looked like a relative," Beth said. "That wouldn't have been—"

"Let's get another photo," Ivy interjected. "I'm not sure we got everyone in the last one." She called out to everyone to gather for another picture.

While Ivy appreciated Beth's generous offer to film, she was still concerned about Shelly's potential promise to her regarding the DNA search and subsequent rights. They had to keep them separated.

Once they'd finished, Shelly hurried away, leaving Ivy with Beth.

"I'd like to introduce my new assistant," Beth said, nodding to a younger man who held camera equipment.

"You look familiar," Ivy said, greeting him.

"I went to high school here," the young man said.

Beth grinned. "I found David online, and he was available for the weekend. You'll hardly know we're here."

Ivy turned to Beth. "I sure appreciate your doing this for Shelly." Keep your friends close, and your enemies closer, she recalled. Not that Beth was an enemy, but Ivy would protect her family.

"I love getting families together," Beth said. "I never had much family. That's why I love doing the show."

Ivy detected a wistfulness in her voice. This was a different side to Beth, which explained a lot. "You're welcome to join in the fun."

Beth glanced at the colorful assortment of hula hoops on the patio and grinned. "Thanks. I might give that a go. It's not something we do in New York very often."

Ivy waited until everyone had gathered. She raised her water glass and tapped it. "Welcome, everyone. I hope you all enjoyed breakfast, courtesy of today's breakfast crew." She gestured to Poppy, Elena, and her daughters to take a bow. "Tomorrow's breakfast crew will be headed by Poppy's brothers, Rocky and Reed, so fair warning to you all."

Amid good-natured comments, the two young men flexed their muscles. "We're beasts in the kitchen," Reed said.

"If you can get yourself out of bed," Elena shot back, ribbing her cousins.

Poppy folded her arms. "I'll make sure my brothers are on time tomorrow. Remember getting doused with cold water? Or that whistle Dad used to use?"

"Speaking of that…" Their father, Forrest, lifted a silver whistle from a chain around his neck. "Got it right here if you want to borrow it."

"I could use that to officiate the games," Sterling said.

"Thought you might." Forrest lifted it over his head and offered it to his father. "I have an extra at the house for Poppy."

"Hey," Rocky protested.

Ivy enjoyed listening to this good-natured sparring. Nearby, her mother and father stood listening, smiling at the chatter as well.

Still, it was time for the games to begin. Ivy clapped her hands to get everyone's attention. "I'm sure our roving patriarch would like to say a few words first."

"Hear, hear!" Rocky called out.

A wave of applause swept across the patio. Sterling raised a hand and blew the whistle.

"Thank you all for that rousing welcome," he said. "It does a man good to know he still has admirers, especially when they're little half-pints like our Daisy."

Carlotta held up Daisy, who cooed at her grandfather. Ivy smiled and took another photo. Daisy had taken an instant liking to Sterling, perhaps realizing he was attached to her beloved grandmother.

"Now, I know this is a competitive bunch, so we must have some ground rules," Sterling said. "This is our first Family Reunion Olympics, and we wouldn't want to interrupt the games with a visit to the emergency room."

"We promise to keep playing, then," Rocky called out, laughing.

Others laughed as well, and Sterling went on. "No hitting, biting, kicking, or any behavior that might result in broken limbs or concussions."

"That sounds like what I used to tell the children," Carlotta remarked, kissing her husband on the cheek.

Sterling grinned. "I thought I'd heard that somewhere before."

As Ivy watched her parents together, a twinge of guilt pinched her. She ran her hand along her neck and thought about the situation with June. She wondered what her parents' response would be. Ivy loved her parents and couldn't imagine that either of them was concealing a secret. However, she was old enough to understand that people made mistakes, or situations might force a course of action that one might think they'd never take.

Bennett's words floated to mind. *Parents are human, too. And like any of us, fallible to a degree at any time.*

The dilemma with June could wait until after the reunion, but she would still meet with the younger woman as promised in the morning.

As she thought of the DNA findings, an unsettling feeling clawed at her. Ivy prided herself on her hospitality to guests and her relationships with friends and family. She realized that was why this was so disturbing.

What if June *should* be here among family?

Her presence would certainly bring a new aspect to the reunion. She wasn't sure how to break this news to her parents yet. She cast a glance at her mother, who was standing with Aunt Maya, chatting easily now.

The two women seemed to have picked up where they left off many years ago. That was the inherent power of family, Ivy decided. But would that be enough for unknown relatives?

Sterling's strong voice rang across the gathering. "Before we begin the tug-o-war rope competition, I want to thank you all for coming. For putting aside schedules, commitments, and..." He paused, his eyes twinkling, and went on, "...even old grudges and misunderstandings to rediscover the joy and meaning of family. In a world where you don't know who you can count on, let's commit to counting on each other."

Speaking with his hand on his heart, Sterling added,

"We're not perfect, but we can be stronger together. May our shared history contribute to our shared futures."

Cheers rang out, and Gabe stepped forward at Sterling's gesture. "Now, to get this party started, Sterling has appointed me captain of one of the tug-of-war teams. I might be an outsider, but I know a good athlete when I see one. You young East Coast ruffians can line up behind me. I'll arrange you in an order as I see fit." He winked. "I've been studying strategy, so you West Coasters should watch out."

A combination of jeers and cheers filled the air.

"Who's the other captain?" Ivy asked, laughing. She was pleased to see everyone looking so happy and eager. Despite her concerns about June, she was enjoying the warmth of her family. Besides the pressing need to reconnect her mother and Aunt Maya, Ivy had been looking forward to this reunion, too.

Honey sauntered forward, her hands on her hips, and faced her husband. "The other team captain, you ask? I'm the *best* captain." She folded her arms with a glint in her eye and turned to Ivy and Bennett. "Let's show my husband what the SoCal Bays are made of. Come on, Ivy. You and Bennett are with me. I slept on the plane, and I'm ready to show my sleep-deprived husband who's the boss. Let's do this."

Sterling blew the whistle. "Let the tug-of-war begin. Line up, folks."

Once the family was split into two teams, they hauled the rope onto the sand amid great shouts and cries and drew a line in the sand. After triple measuring to make sure the distance and rope lengths were fair, the two teams lined up on opposite sides of the line.

Ivy loved the camaraderie and good-natured kidding she'd known in childhood, growing up in a rambunctious family. None of her siblings were perfect, but they were perfect together in their imperfect way.

She smiled to herself at the thought.

Honey positioned her team. Along with her daughter

Elena, she had chosen Flint's boys, Skyler and Blue, while Gabe called for Maya's son Robert and his boys, who had arrived late last night and driven from the Los Angeles airport. Diana and Robert's children were around her children's ages. Thankfully, they were having fun with their new-found cousins.

Bennett took his place behind Ivy. "I hope you're ready to go against that crew over there."

"I'm definitely up for it." Ivy winked. "We all are." She loved that Bennett was participating. Jeremy had been too proper and preoccupied to join in family festivities like this. They had also invited Bennett's sister Kendra and her husband Dave. Their son Logan had another event, but they would all join them later at the tacky tourist party this evening.

At last, Sterling held up his hand. "On your mark, get set, go," he yelled, followed by a screech of the whistle.

"Go team!" Honey cried. "Dig in and pull!"

"Here we go," Ivy added, gripping the sturdy rope. Immediately, she and Bennett were swept into the enthusiasm. She dug her heels into the soft sand and leaned back with all her might. "Keep pulling," she yelled.

The teams were well-matched, and each side proved a worthy competitor. The advantage shifted from one side to another, but in the end, Honey's team successfully pulled the opposition over the line. People tumbled onto the sand, laughing, and Ivy and Bennett were among them.

"Hey, watch out for your elders," Ivy said, laughing. The younger guys were rough-housing, and Bennett and Mitch joined in, though she steered clear of their enthusiasm.

Even Daisy got in on the action from the sidelines, laughing and waving her hands with glee at the happy melee. Carlotta held Daisy up so she could see, and the little one squealed with delight.

Taking Ivy's hands, Bennett helped her to her feet. He

gazed at her with fresh admiration. "Wow, I haven't seen you this competitive in sports before."

"Against my family? You bet I am," she replied, laughing. "We all are. When we were kids, my parents used to organize silly games like this for us. Later, they admitted it was partly to wear us out, so we'd sleep well. But we all had such fun and made wonderful memories."

"So that's where you get your determination and competitive spirit."

Ivy glanced at her parents, who stood watching their family with arms around each other's waists. "Mom and Dad are to thank for that. Mom taught us perseverance, and Dad showed us the joy in winning and the grace in losing. Although my brothers are still working on that last part."

"Hey," Flint cried. "I resemble that remark."

Ivy laughed and elbowed her brother. "Get out of here with your corny old jokes and come up with some new material."

Next to them, Poppy dusted sand from her knees. "Looks like the family Olympics are off to a good start."

"Thanks to you," Ivy said, slinging an arm over her niece's shoulder.

Poppy looked pleased. "We all worked together."

The rest of the day was filled with fun and laughter as two groups tied for the win in the relay race, the younger women trounced the men in beach volleyball, and everyone had a blast with the hula hoops.

Darla joined Aunt Maya and Diana to watch from the patio until Sterling was finally able to talk Diana into participating in the hula contest. Maybe it was her father's charm or Shelly's Sea Breeze cocktails, but Diana's haughty, brittle attitude finally cracked. By the end of the hula contest, she and Beth were laughing together at their efforts.

Later that afternoon, Ivy and Bennett dressed for the evening's tacky tourist party. She wore a gaudy rhinestone hat, a belted pack with assorted travel gear dangling from it, and neon-bright, clashing clothes. She rounded the corner to the bedroom as Bennett was getting ready. "How are you doing in here?"

He held out his arms. "What do you think?"

Ivy laughed. "I don't know which I like better, the fishing hat or the mismatched socks with flip-flops." The hat was covered with lures, and he'd paired a Hawaiian shirt with camo shorts and Christmas-themed socks—Rudolph the red-nosed reindeer on one knee sock and a snowman on the other.

"What a pair we make," he said, chuckling. "Let's go see what everyone else came up with."

The scene was festive, with all sorts of ridiculous outfits and silly hats. Mitch had organized a Mexican buffet with quesadillas, nachos, guacamole, salad, and enchiladas. He wore a torn surfer T-shirt and scuba goggles on his head, while Shelly wore a sarong with hiking boots.

Poppy and the other cousins had organized playlists of vintage Beach Boys, Jimmy Buffett, Bob Marley, and other beach party music. The younger cousins started dancing, and Ivy and Bennett joined in as others crowded the patio outside.

"Hey, you're not bad," Ivy said as Bennett slipped his arms around her and swayed when *The Girl from Ipanema* came on.

"Take a look at your parents," Bennett said. He twirled her around to see them.

Carlotta and Sterling were dancing in perfect rhythm to the bossa nova beat, and the family made room for them, whistling and clapping.

"They've had years of experience," Ivy said.

"We'll be like that someday." Bennett's eyes brightened. "How would you feel about dance lessons? I'd love to spin you around the dance floor like that."

"You're not so bad." Ivy smiled. The light pressure of his hand on her back felt nice, and she loved dancing close to him. Her husband had a natural rhythm, and she enjoyed this, even though they didn't do it nearly often enough. "If you're serious, I think dance lessons would be fun."

"We need something extra in our lives," Bennett said. "Something that's just you and me. As much as I like having guests, family, and friends coming and going at all hours, we need our time, too." He smiled at her and added, "We could dance on that honeymoon we're planning."

"Are we? I seem to have forgotten where we're going." A speck of guilt pinched her neck.

"Wherever you want, sweetheart." As the song came to an end, Bennett leaned down and kissed her softly.

Ivy warmed to his touch. "This just became the best reunion ever." She loved the feeling of his arms around her. "Maybe we can take that trip sooner than I thought," Ivy said, leaning her head against Bennett's chest.

"I'd like nothing more."

She smiled up at him. "I'd love for us to end up just like my parents."

"I know we will," Bennett said, kissing her again.

His kiss was so sweet that Ivy almost forgot about June and the situation they would have to figure out in the morning.

At a break in the music, Sterling and Carlotta gathered everyone to give out awards.

"To the farthest traveled," Sterling began. "Our cousin Robert and his family from the East Coast. For the tackiest tourist costumes, it's Bennett for third place, Elena for second place, and Rocky for first place," Sterling announced a few other awards amid wild applause and whistles. "Come on up, all of you."

As they lined up, Beth kept the camera running. She and her assistant had been filming all day, and Ivy was glad that she was a good sport about it.

Imani had drafted an email for Shelly in case she encountered any issues with Beth. Ivy had to trust that Shelly would take care of that. Still, she couldn't help wondering if this was really how Beth wanted to spend her vacation. Beth was more of a Hamptons-type of person, despite what she'd shared about her background.

After the awards, Mitch served cupcakes for dessert, and Poppy turned up the music again. Ivy noticed Shelly at a table off to one side, rocking Daisy in her arms. She joined her sister.

"How is Daisy sleeping through this?" Ivy asked.

"I think she's worn out from overstimulation. I'll tuck her into her portable carrier, and we'll take her home soon."

"What an incredibly fun day this has been." Ivy stretched, rubbing her sore arm muscles from the volleyball game.

Shelly stifled a yawn. "I wonder how long this will go on."

"The cousins are young, but it's been a long day." She hesitated, not wanting to spoil the vibe, but she had to ask. "I've been thinking about our meeting with June in the morning."

"Me, too." Shelly turned to her. "What if all this is for real?"

"It might very well be. DNA doesn't lie. Although labs have been known to mix up results. It's rare, but it does happen."

"She looks a lot like us."

Ivy nodded. "I see that, too. I didn't want to at first, but she really does."

"Then June ought to be here with us. She could meet everyone at once."

Ivy shot a warning look at her sister. "We need to figure out exactly how she's related first. It could be awfully uncomfortable—for everyone."

"Maybe someone donated some sperm to a sperm bank." Shelly brightened. "Then it would be cool, right? No fault at all."

Her sister had a point. "I hadn't thought of that," Ivy said slowly. "I've also been thinking about how June must feel. And her mother. I wonder what it's like not knowing your ancestry."

Shelly nodded thoughtfully. "And then discovering the possibility of a big family nearby." She hesitated. "I feel a little selfish about that. As if we're keeping our good fortune of having a great family from her."

"I've been thinking that, too. June seems earnest about connecting, but she also seems wary. Maybe she's unsure about being accepted." Ivy tucked an edge of the baby blanket around Daisy's exposed toes as she weighed their options. "If we can figure this out, what do you think about approaching Mom and Dad and asking for their permission to include June and her mother?"

"Depending on the history." Pausing, Shelly smiled with relief. "I'm glad you're not mad at me anymore."

Ivy bumped her shoulder. "Whatever happened back then wasn't your fault. Still, we need to deal with this situation now. If someone has been harboring a secret, maybe they'll be relieved it's out. Look at how Mom and Aunt Maya are getting along now."

"That's a good intention, but it might backfire on us," Shelly said.

"You sound like me now."

"I've been thinking about it a lot, too. I'm excited, but I don't want to hurt anyone."

Ivy let out a long sigh. It was time to come to terms with the past. "That's a chance we have to take."

a tap sounded at the door to the apartment, and Ivy hurried to answer it. "June is early," Ivy said to Shelly, who had joined her this morning after a late breakfast. Daisy was sleeping beside her in a portable carrier.

"Hi," Beth said brightly. "I thought you might like to capture this meeting on film. It would be great on the show."

For a moment, Ivy was flummoxed. "How did you know about this?"

Beth darted a look at Shelly, who rose quickly.

"Thanks for staying on," Shelly cut in. "But I told you last night, this is personal."

Beth frowned with annoyance. "You asked for my help with the DNA search," she said pointedly. "And you wanted me to film the reunion, so here we are." She motioned to an assistant behind her, who carried camera equipment.

Ivy started to reply, but Shelly took a step forward. "No, you offered to film the reunion, and I accepted. This meeting is outside of those parameters."

Ivy suppressed a grin. Clearly, Shelly had read Imani's email and taken her advice to heart.

But Beth wasn't backing down. "You signed a release."

"About that," Shelly said sweetly. "I sent you an email from my attorney that should clear up everything. She reviewed the documents."

Ivy smiled, proud of her sister. "We're so glad you're enjoying your holiday here, Beth. We can chat later, but we're expecting someone now."

"I can't believe you're passing up this opportunity to be on TV," Beth said to Shelly. "It could make your career and take you back to New York. Do you know what people do to get on the *Family Archives?*"

Shelly put her arm around Ivy. "We're not like most people. Some things are only for us. And as for my career, I'm happy right where I am."

Beth shook her head in disgust and turned to her assistant. "We're out of here."

After Shelly shut the door firmly behind Beth, Ivy turned to her. "Well done."

A smile grew on Shelly's face. "You're not the only one who inherited Mom's determination. As for Beth, she's okay, but she's not a real friend. She just wanted a segment at our expense."

"It's a shame," Ivy said. "Because I think there's a genuine person somewhere in there."

A few minutes later, June arrived. In her hands, she clutched an envelope.

"Welcome back." Ivy motioned for her to sit on the sofa. She served coffee while June and Shelly spoke.

"I don't have much time, but I think this might be important," June said as she opened the envelope and withdrew a folded document. "This is my mother's birth certificate." She blushed slightly. "She doesn't know I took this today."

"Does she live nearby?" Ivy asked. That might change how they handled this situation.

"Mom lives on Crown Island, too," June replied.

Ivy took the birth certificate and read it. "This has been amended."

"Yes, as I mentioned," June said. "Still, we think the birth-date is correct because my grandmother says my mother was a newborn when she came to them."

"That's important," Ivy said, noting the date. That could help confirm the relationship.

"There's more," June said, taking out a thin necklace from which dangled a gold heart. "When my grandparents adopted my mother, the nuns gave them this."

Ivy leaned forward. "May I see that?"

"Of course." June passed it to her.

One side was smooth, and Ivy turned it over. A rose was engraved on the other side. The gold was still bright—it looked like a higher gold content that was more common in Europe. But it was the design that intrigued her.

"I've seen this before," Ivy said slowly. "Recently, I discov-ered a sketch of a woman who wore a necklace like this. My mother and aunt say it was their sister. But she died in an automobile accident."

"I wonder how common this design was," Shelly said, leaning over to look at it.

June looked quizzical. "What was her name?"

"Pilar Reina." Ivy shook her head. "I'm sorry, but I just don't see how it would have been possible."

"Maybe Pilar borrowed the necklace," Shelly said. "Or, what if it was someone else's?"

Ivy touched Shelly's hand. "I think it's time we told Mom about this. She might have some answers." She handed the necklace back to June.

The younger woman seemed flustered. "Will your mother be upset?"

Ivy and Shelly looked at each other. "Our mother isn't like that," Ivy said. "Surprised, maybe. But I promise we'll figure this out. You and your mother deserve some answers." And so do we, Ivy thought.

"When will you speak to her?"

Ivy quickly revised her thoughts. "Given that necklace, the sooner, the better."

Shelly's eyes loomed large in her face. "It might be easier to figure out with everyone here."

Slowly, Ivy nodded. Rather than agonizing over this situation, they could resolve it, and perhaps more quickly than they realized. An idea formed in her mind. "Would you excuse me for a few minutes?"

June's eyes were bright. "Of course, but my mother is waiting for me in the car. May I bring her in? We had a special lunch planned, but I told her I needed to drop something here. She's talking to a friend on the phone."

"That's fine," Ivy said. She was curious to meet June's mother, too. "And may I borrow that necklace for a few minutes?"

IVY MADE her way upstairs in the main house to her former room and knocked on the door. "Mom, Dad, may I come in?"

Her mother opened the door. "Your father isn't here, but Maya and I are having coffee and catching up."

The two women sat in a pair of vintage wingback chairs that Ivy had slip-covered in heavy white cotton and positioned by the window to overlook the sea.

"I hope you don't think we're being anti-social, although I have been guilty of that," Maya said.

Carlotta smiled and clasped her sister's hand. "We have so much to catch up on that we might bore others around us. We've been remembering our sister Pilar today."

Ivy knew they needed this time to share memories. She was pleased that her mother and aunt were getting along so well—they reminded her of herself and Shelly.

In the pocket of her sundress, Ivy curled her hand around the small necklace. She was so happy for them that she feared bringing up this potentially life-altering news, but she also felt it was her duty.

"Mom, I brought something to show you and Aunt Maya. I'm not sure what to make of it."

"Well, what is it?" Carlotta asked.

Her heart pounding, Ivy brought out the heart-shaped necklace. "Does this look familiar?"

Carlotta shook her head, but Maya reached for it. "I haven't seen one like this in years." She turned it over and stared at the engraved rose. "Flavio gave one like this to Pilar. She hid it from our parents, but she showed it to me. They planned to engrave their names or initials on one side."

"I recognized it from the sketch," Ivy said. Now, she was certain they must meet.

"Where did you find this?" Maya asked.

Ivy perched on the arm of her mother's chair and put her arm across her shoulders. "This is going to sound awfully far-fetched, but Shelly and I need your help." As she looked at her mother and aunt, the resemblance between them and June came into focus. She could only imagine what June's mother would look like.

"Would you mind joining Shelly and me for a few minutes?" Ivy asked, trying to rein in her eagerness. "We have two guests I think you'll want to meet. We can talk over a fresh cup of coffee in my quarters."

20

*W*hen Ivy opened the door to the apartment, she saw that June's mother had joined Shelly and June in the living room. The attractive woman looked a little older than Ivy. She wore a lovely pastel floral sundress and with her wavy brown hair and green eyes, she clearly favored the rest of the family gathered here.

More than ever, Ivy was noticing the physical resemblance, yet they needed to determine how they were related. Maybe it was through her grandfather, Ivy suddenly thought. It might even make sense that he would have given away the necklace. She could only imagine how painful it would have been to keep it, especially given the circumstances of Pilar's death.

June gestured to the woman with her. "This is my mother, April. I told her what I've shared with you."

"I'm so happy to meet you," Ivy said. She leaned the sketch she had picked up on the way here against the wall before introducing Carlotta and Aunt Maya. While they talked, she made her way into the kitchen and put on coffee for the small group.

Shelly began first, "After our baby was born, my husband and I decided to have our DNA analyzed to see if we might have genetic issues to watch for in Daisy. What we didn't expect was to find a relative we didn't know anything about. And we can't figure out how we might be related."

Ivy watched June's mother, who seemed nervous. Surely this was difficult for her, too. Ivy was glad her daughter was with her.

June took her mother's hand. "Mom asked me to share our side of the story with you. She was adopted, but it was a closed adoption. This discovery has been quite emotional for her. I told her a little bit just now."

"I appreciate your understanding," April said, placing a slender hand over her heart. "Of all days, this is certainly a surprise. I didn't even know my daughter had done a DNA search."

"I'm sorry I didn't tell you," June said. "But I thought another dead end would be upsetting to you."

April acknowledged that with a slight nod. "When I was younger, I was very curious about my parents and my ancestry, but I've gone so long without answers that I'd given up hope. You might wonder why it mattered to me because I had a very happy childhood. But I always felt there was a missing connection. I suppose I wanted to know why I was given away." She hesitated, drawing in a long breath. "However, I was confident that I could understand my birth mother's decision in retrospect. Basically, I sought to understand my personal history."

June spoke up again. "My mother taught history, so she has a natural curiosity about the past."

"June tells me you're having a family reunion," April said. "We don't mean to crash the party. We're simply curious, and I assure you, we want nothing from you."

Ivy liked this woman immediately. April had an innate grace that was evident in her daughter as well. Even if they weren't in this situation, the two women were ones she might be friends with. As the coffee gurgled to completion, she poured the steaming brew for those who wanted it.

Shelly went on, "There's the DNA, but there's more." She nodded toward Ivy.

"I found this sketch a few days ago." Ivy lifted the sketch and turned it around. "And yesterday, we learned this is our aunt, Pilar. The middle sister to my mother and aunt. If you're related to us, then you're probably related to her, too."

April leaned forward, staring at the sketch.

Ivy noticed that Carlotta and Maya were also watching April. Ivy held up the gold necklace. "This necklace that June showed us looks like the one Pilar is wearing."

Aunt Maya turned to April. "Our sister's boyfriend, Flavio, gave her the necklace. He was also a talented artist, as you can see."

April studied the sketch. Finally, she nodded. "It looks quite similar."

"Mom is also an artist," June said. "She makes beautiful pottery."

"It's just a hobby," April said, still staring at the sketch. She was clearly moved. A few moments later, she opened her purse and brought out a smaller coin purse. From that, she withdrew a handkerchief, cupping it in her hands as if it was her greatest treasure in the world. "What was Pilar's last name?"

Carlotta smiled. "Our family name is Reina."

"P.R.," April whispered. Silent tears welled in her eyes. She held out a delicate, white linen handkerchief that was folded into quarters.

Carlotta took the lace-trimmed square of fabric from her. She looked at it with vague recognition and showed it to her sister. "We used to make ones quite similar to this."

Motioning to her, April said, "Unfold it."

As Carlotta opened the old handkerchief, surprise filled Maya's face. She touched the embroidered stitches with reverence. "I remember this."

Ivy looked over their shoulders at the monogram. "P.R. Pilar Reina?"

Tears glistened in Maya's eyes. "Pilar never had the patience for embroidery, so I helped her finish it. See, these small stitches are mine, and the longer ones are hers. She was always in a hurry to go outside and play." When Maya looked up, a flash of understanding swept across her face.

Ivy felt it, too. "Let's look at the birth certificate," she said quickly, holding out her hand. She hardly dared to hope, even though all signs pointed to this new truth.

June handed it to her, and Ivy passed it to her mother. "This is April's. Do you recognize the birthdate?" she asked softly.

Carlotta scanned the old document and pointed to the birthdate. Her eyes widened with astonishment. "Oh, my goodness. That's today."

"How could that be?" Aunt Maya pressed a hand to her heart.

"There's only one explanation," Carlotta said, her voice quavering. She clutched her sister's hand, and their faces were filled with wonder and joy.

Carlotta turned to the little group that leaned forward with anticipation. "April, today you celebrate your birthday. And today, we honor our sister, for this is the day she left us. At the time, she was nearly nine months pregnant." She held a hand out to April.

April pressed her hands to her cheeks, unable to speak at the realization.

Ivy caught her breath. *Was it really so?*

Shelly looked between Carlotta and Ivy. "But I thought Pilar and her baby died in the accident. Does this mean what I think it does?"

"You unlocked a long-lost secret." Ivy smiled at her mother, Aunt Maya, and April, who were embracing each other. All were crying tears of joy. "Pilar was lost, but the doctors must have managed to save her baby girl. April's birth was the day Pilar died. So, she is truly one of us. As is June."

Carlotta held April in her arms. "You are the daughter of our beloved sister, which makes you our precious niece. How we wish we'd known you survived."

"I wonder if our parents knew," Aunt Maya said.

Carlotta shook her head. "Mother never would have given you up."

Slowly, Aunt Maya nodded. "She and Father grieved Pilar's death so deeply. This was probably a decision made by the nuns and doctor. Back then, they often did what they thought best for the families. April, your parents might have been eagerly awaiting your birth."

"Yes, I believe they were."

"Our grandparents must have thought Pilar's illegitimate baby would hurt her sister's chance for a good match." Aunt Maya shook her head. "The pressure from Mother's parents is why Pilar was sent away, but Mother insisted she stay close. Here, at the inn, which at the time was known as Las Brisas del Mar and owned by Mother's good friend."

"Sterling wouldn't have cared," Carlotta said. "For us, it was love at first sight."

"But his family might have objected," Maya reminded her.

Stepping forward, Ivy touched April's back. "That makes you and your daughter our cousins. Welcome to the family. We have so much history to share with you."

April embraced her. "I'd like that so very much." She held a hand to June. "And my daughter, June. I have another daughter who is traveling. You'll meet May when she returns."

Ivy watched the scene unfold before her, hardly believing what they had pieced together. "I'm so glad you had the courage to contact us. For that alone, I know you're truly part of us. We're quite a determined bunch."

"Not that we haven't made a lot of mistakes," Shelly added with a grin.

June nodded at that. "You have no idea how much we share that trait."

As Ivy pieced together the details to her satisfaction, she decided the only thing that remained was how to tell the rest of the family. She hoped the family would accept April and June, especially Diana and her brother. Turning to June and April, she asked, "Do you have plans later today?"

"We do," June replied. "I had already planned to take my mother to lunch in Summer Beach to see an old friend, Ginger Delavie. This is an incredible bonus that I couldn't have even imagined." She clasped her mother's hand.

Carlotta's face brightened at the mention of Ginger. "What a small world. Ginger and I have been friends for many years. She's treasured here in Summer Beach. If you'd like, please invite her to our luau tonight on my behalf. She's always welcome here."

"You'll have a chance to meet everyone at once," Ivy said, her heart filled with happiness for June and her mother. "We'd love for you to join us."

April's eyes sparkled. "We'd like that very much. We're meeting Ginger at the Coral Cottage, so if she's available, we'll bring her to the luau with us. She'll be just as surprised as we are."

"Everyone will be," Ivy said. "We'll say a few words and introduce you this evening. Shelly's husband has planned a special menu, and if you'd like to dress for the luau, please do."

"This sounds so exciting," June said.

Ivy thought so, too. It would be an event to remember. In a good way, she hoped.

21

"*A*loha," Ivy said, greeting family members arriving for the luau on the patio. Everyone had risen to the occasion, decked out in all manner of Hawaiian outfits. Bennett's sister and her husband were there with their son Logan. The little boy beamed at her, and she told him how much she liked his aloha shirt.

"There's plenty of food," she added, greeting Kendra and Dave. "Help yourselves."

"My brother said he's cooking tonight," Kendra said with an arched eyebrow.

Ivy laughed at her sister-in-law's expression of mock horror. "Under Mitch's tutelage, of course. But Bennett has become a pretty good cook, too."

"Sure smells good," Dave said.

"And the decorations are lovely," Kendra said, steering her hungry son toward the food.

Ivy was pleased with the luau decorations that Poppy and her cousins had organized. Bamboo tiki torches and paper lanterns created a soft glow on this balmy evening. Tropical red ginger flowers and leaves decorated the tables, which were trimmed with raffia skirts that rustled in the soft ocean breeze.

Music from local Hawaiian artists filled the air, and Ivy hummed to Israel Kamakawiwo'ole's version of *Over the Rainbow*.

While chatting with family members, Ivy kept an eye out for June and her mother, who would be arriving soon.

The party was turning out even better than she had imagined. Everyone had gotten in the mood with colorful shirts and sarongs. Her mother and Aunt Maya were wearing long cotton muumuu dresses with island prints they'd found at a shop in the village. Ivy wore a pikake-print sundress with one of the fragrant leis that Imani had provided for them. The scent was heavenly.

She glanced at the time. When June and her mother arrived, Ivy would begin the important announcement. Her nerves were on edge, and she was unsure if everyone would accept them as part of the family. What if someone questioned their right to be there? If anyone did, it would be Diana, Ivy imagined. She didn't know if Aunt Maya planned to tell her children or not.

One thing was certain. The presence of June and April would certainly change the dynamics.

In the meantime, Ivy took a plate and filled it with appetizers—or a pupu platter, as it was called in Hawaii. She loved the grilled pineapple and pulled pork that Mitch made.

Her friend Leilani Miyake waved at her.

"What do you think of how the food turned out?" Ivy asked.

"Mitch takes direction well. This is as authentic as he can get without a full imu ceremony in the islands."

"The guys will be glad to hear you approve."

Leilani and her husband Roy owned the Hidden Garden nursery and had advised Mitch on the menu. The couple was from Hawaii and spent winters there with family. With their help, Mitch had created a menu featuring pulled pork, pork ribs, and chicken wings, along with coconut shrimp and poke. For the vegetarians, he had prepared vegetable skewers, grilled pineapple, fried rice balls, and plenty of mango salsa. The fruit platter was filled with tropical offerings, including dragon fruit, starfruit, papaya, guava, and mangoes. Mitch had prepped the dishes, and he and Bennett were taking turns at the grill.

Bennett winked at her. She'd told him all about the plan to introduce June and April, and he'd been supportive. "What do you think of the food?" he asked.

Ivy gestured to her plate. "This was full a few minutes ago." She smiled, admiring her husband, who looked good in the chef jacket Mitch had supplied. "It's all delicious. Everyone loves what you've done."

"Mitch is the brains behind it," Bennett said, grinning.

Not far from them, Poppy was managing the bar. She had coerced her brothers Rocky and Reed to help her make mai tais and POG Delight—a non-alcoholic concoction of papaya, orange, and guava juices. The pineapple wine from Maui Poppy was serving was also a refreshing favorite with many in the family.

Sipping on a juice drink, Shelly sauntered toward her wearing a vibrant sarong. "The guys are sure serving up a good dinner."

"They seem to be a huge hit," Ivy replied.

"That smells so good," Aunt Maya said, joining them with her daughter Diana. She glanced at Ivy's plate. "What do you call that?"

"Delicious," Ivy said, grinning. As she nibbled, she explained the menu to Aunt Maya and Diana.

Maya sipped a mai tai. "This reminds me of the parties our parents used to have when I was young. They loved Hawaii, and we traveled there often."

"Have you tried the appetizers from the pupu platter?" Shelly asked.

"Carlotta brought a few to me," Maya replied. "Did you have all this catered?"

Shelly gestured with pride toward the grill. "My husband made everything." Behind her, Mitch listened in, grinning.

"Aren't you the lucky one?" Maya said. "I've been watching Mitch with Daisy. He's an attentive father—and a talented chef. Carlotta and I visited Java Beach, and I must admit, the coffee was excellent. Mitch certainly passes muster in my book. Bennett, too."

Shelly beamed, and Ivy knew she and Mitch were relieved. Even though Bennett wasn't generally concerned with what people thought of him, he was trying to make a good impression for her sake, too.

"Are we almost ready for the big announcement?" Maya asked.

"They should be here any minute," Ivy replied. Although she was trying to remain calm, her nerves were doing a cha-cha.

Her aunt's expression softened. "April and June remind me so much of Pilar. I'd like to get to know them better before I leave."

"You'll have to return soon," Ivy said. And this time, she meant it. She'd discovered a different side to her aunt and her side of the family.

Maya pressed a hand on Ivy's shoulder. "I'd like that. Next time, I'm sure I can manage on my own. I'm sorry I was so difficult in the beginning."

"I understand, and it's completely forgotten." She embraced her aunt. "I'm so glad we've reunited."

After Maya moved on to speak to Carlotta, Shelly whispered to Ivy, "Are you nervous?"

"A little. I'm glad we have the support of Mom and Aunt Maya." She smiled at her sister. "You look great tonight, by the way."

Shelly gestured to her purple batik-print, wrap-around

skirt that she'd paired with a tank top. "These sarongs are so easy to wear. I can also cross and wrap the ends around my neck and wear it as a dress."

"It's pretty, but that's not what I mean. You look relaxed and happy. Are you feeling better?"

"A lot," Shelly said. "I feel like every day is a little bit sunnier. There are more good days than bad days now—many more, in fact. Maybe it's seeing everyone again, or maybe it's the therapy and yoga."

"Probably all of it. And you're getting more sleep." Ivy was glad to see the clouds of Shelly's postpartum depression dissipating.

"Daisy has slept so soundly the last couple of nights. I hope that's a new trend." Shelly waggled her fingers at her across the patio. Carlotta was carrying her daughter, showing her off to the relatives, and Daisy was gurgling with laughter.

Just then, Ivy spied June and her mother by the door. Their mutual friend, Ginger Delavie, was with them. Ivy was pleased that Ginger had accompanied them for moral support. After motioning to her mother and aunt, she made her way toward June and greeted them. The three women were wearing Hawaiian dresses, and they'd received leis on the way in.

"Are you ready?" Ivy asked.

"We're a little nervous," June said. "Especially Mom."

April's face was flushed. "This is a day I thought would never come."

"It's going to be fine," Ivy said. "We'll make an announcement, and then you're officially one of us. Get ready for a barrage of questions."

"And hugs," Carlotta added, joining them with Maya. "We're a hugging sort of family."

"This is so exciting," Ginger whispered, clasping hands with Carlotta and April. "Imagine discovering that two of my favorite people are related. Why, I'm surprised I didn't make the connection before. The resemblance is so strong. Aunt and niece, am I correct?"

"That's right," Carlotta said. "We have so much to share with April and June about our dear Pilar and our parents."

"I can hardly wait," April said. "This was the best birthday gift I could have imagined. I have so many questions about our family." Her face was filled with wonder and gratitude.

Ivy looked at the crowd. "I think most people have finished eating. Shall we do this now?"

"We're ready," June replied.

Ivy tapped on a glass to get everyone's attention. "We have an announcement to make. And a very special surprise."

The five women joined hands—Ivy, Shelly, Carlotta, June, and April. Ivy's father held Daisy, who was enamored with her grandfather now.

"Recently, we've had an exciting development in our family," Ivy began. "Shelly and Mitch had their DNA analyzed for Daisy's sake. And a surprising discovery was made." She paused and turned to June and April. "You might wonder who these two lovely women are with us."

June and April looked out over the crowd with nervous smiles.

Ivy continued, "Some of you know that my mother and Aunt Maya had a sister who passed away in an auto accident at a young age. What you don't know is that Pilar was pregnant. And until recently, none of us knew that Pilar's baby survived. What's even more intriguing is that my grandmother placed Pilar here at the Seabreeze Inn—then called Las Brisas del Mar—under the protection of her good friend, Amelia Erickson." As soon as Ivy said that, the exterior lights blinked a couple of times.

Their relatives gasped and murmurs swept across the patio.

"Looks like Amelia approves," Shelly said. Laughter

rippled throughout the family, and people began asking questions.

"Yes, Pilar's daughter is with us today," Ivy said. "Let's all give a big family welcome to Pilar's daughter April and her daughter June."

"Woo-hoo!" Shelly called out, clapping. She hugged April and June, and other family members began to greet them as well.

Even Diana, who held back at first, approached with her brother and their children to welcome June and April. "This trip has certainly been full of surprises. Ivy, I'm sorry if I came off a little brusque when I arrived. I'd forgotten how much fun it is to be part of a big, extended family."

"Traveling can be challenging," Ivy said. "But I'm so glad we got to know each other." Diana and Robert weren't so bad after all; in fact, Ivy had found common ground in talking about their families.

April held up her hand. "I couldn't have asked for a better welcome into the family that I've been searching for most of my adult life. That many of you live so close, and that we even have a mutual friend is astounding. Ginger Delavie is here with us tonight."

Standing next to her, Ginger acknowledged a few people she knew here. "I can assure you that April is a fine person. You're fortunate to have found each other."

"My daughter June arranged all this for me as a surprise today, which is my birthday," April said. "And I'd love for you to meet my other daughter, May, who is traveling right now. She's eager to meet you all as well."

Ivy stepped back to watch family members greet April and June. She looked at Bennett, who was making his way to her.

When he reached her side, he put his arm around her. "Once again, you've surprised me with the way you handled this situation."

"It wasn't easy at first," she said. "There was a lot to sort out. If Mom and Aunt Maya hadn't been here, we couldn't have really confirmed our mutual history. But look at everyone now. They're all fascinated with this new connection."

"The reunion has been a success, too. I know how much you wanted to do this for your parents."

"They look like they're enjoying themselves." Ivy leaned against Bennett's sturdy frame. His support and acknowledgment meant so much to her. "I couldn't have planned such a perfect surprise; it was as if an unseen hand was guiding us. We wouldn't have discovered the sketch unless Diana had come early."

Bennett grinned and kissed her forehead. "Maybe it was the spirit of Amelia Erickson?"

Ivy smiled up at her husband. "Something like that." She was almost ready to believe, but not quite.

LATER THAT EVENING, the family gathered on the beach in front of the firepit, reminiscing and laughing as they shared stories with their newest members, June and April.

Leaning forward to warm her hands against the evening chill, Ivy watched the pair across the flickering fire. So far, they were meshing well with the family.

"Do you like living on Crown Island?" Shelly asked.

"It's a wonderful community," April replied. "Much like Summer Beach, and not that far away." She glanced at her daughter. "June has just returned to Crown Island. You might say that we're both starting new chapters in our lives."

June dipped her head. "They don't want to hear about our challenges, Mom."

Ivy's curiosity was piqued. "Shelly and I started over in Summer Beach, and it wasn't that long ago." She slipped her hand into Bennett's. "That was one of the best moves of our lives."

"I'd like to hear more about how you accomplished that,"

April said. "We're doing okay, but we're both on our own for the first time in years. That's why discovering all of you means so much to us."

April's words struck Ivy, and she detected a raw vulnerability under the other woman's brave, gracious exterior. "Whenever you'd like to talk, we're here." More than discovering new cousins, Ivy felt like she'd found new friends.

April smiled at Carlotta and Maya, who were sitting next to her in Adirondack chairs. "For now, I want to learn more about my mother and her sisters. What was Pilar like as a child?"

"She had a magnetic smile...the most fun and outgoing one of us." Carlotta gazed into the fire, recalling her memories. "Maya, remember the time that she talked our parents into adopting a dog?"

As they reminisced, April and June leaned forward, listening to every word. Ivy noticed a few yawns around the firepit.

Sitting next to Carlotta, Sterling motioned toward their quarters. "Why don't you two turn in? We won't be much longer."

Ivy kissed her father on the cheek. "Thanks, Dad. It's been a long day." She and Bennett slipped away from the family. When they reached their unit, Ivy strolled onto the open-air deck.

Bennett swept his arms around her. "Care for a glass of wine in the treehouse?"

"I'd love that." While Bennett opened a bottle, Ivy lit a few candles. The rustle of palm fronds and rhythmic ocean waves was the only soundtrack they needed. Ivy nestled on the sofa as Bennett poured two glasses.

Touching her glass, he said, "Here's to you, and to family." As they sipped, Bennett draped his arm around her shoulders. "I have a confession to make."

The serious tone of his voice struck her. "I'm listening."

"I've been wondering lately if our lives could be more adventurous. At times I've questioned if I was missing out on something."

Ivy grew quiet. Between the demands of the mayoral office and the inn, had their lives become too predictable? "Is there anything I can do to help?"

Bennett drew her closer. "I didn't realize what being part of the Bay and Reina families meant before the reunion. Your extended family made me and Mitch feel so much a part of them."

Ivy enjoyed hearing that. She'd watched how Bennett built trust and friendship with others in her family. "What do you think now?"

"I fell in love with you," Bennett replied, cradling her cheek in his palm. "But now I feel like I discovered the real heart of a sprawling family. The traditions, history, and love between you all touched me on a deep level. The way you brought April and June into the family—and Kendra, Dave, and Logan, too—recalibrated my thoughts."

"And now?"

"Sometimes a man looks at the other side of the fence, at friends who have bigger boats like Tyler and his buddies who are building important businesses and taking trips around the world."

"We should have a chance to travel more someday. Is that what you'd like to do?" Ivy asked softly.

Bennett shook his head. "These last few days showed me that there's more to life than the proverbial bigger boat. Not that there's anything wrong with that, but I have all I could want right here. The love of my life and the love of her family. I'm so grateful for that—what more could I ask for?"

His words meant so much to her. Ivy ran her hand over his shoulder. "Dance lessons?"

Laughing, Bennett said, "We don't have to do that."

"You've gotten me all excited for nothing? No, sir. We're

signing up. I'm going to waltz and foxtrot with you if it's the last thing I do. We can dance on the beach."

"We've already done that, remember?"

Ivy rested her head on Bennett's shoulder. "I'll never forget that night. But learning how to dance with you would be fun. Look at Mom and Dad and how much they enjoy dancing together."

"Well, then, I know just the place in town," Bennett said, his eyes twinkling in the candlelight.

"And there's one more thing I've been thinking about." She knew what had been on his mind for a long time, and she wanted to meet him halfway. That's what marriage was all about. Creating family bonds, being there for each other, and realizing their dreams together. "About that honeymoon… how about this winter?"

Bennett looked surprised. "Are you sure you can get away?"

"I'll make the time." She pressed a hand to his cheek, resolving to keep her promise to him.

He kissed her on the forehead. "Where did you have in mind?"

Ivy tilted her face to her husband, teasing him with her lips. "You'll never guess."

Bennett threw his head back and laughed. "Probably not. But this is what I love about you, Ivy Bay. You keep our future exciting."

"And I love everything about you." She twined her arms around his neck, enjoying the connection between them.

As they found themselves in each other's arms, their wine was quickly forgotten. Their future lay ahead, and Ivy was certain now that whatever happened, their love would only grow.

The End

AUTHOR'S NOTE

Thank you for reading *Seabreeze Reunion*, and I hope you enjoyed the reunion at the Seabreeze Inn. Find out what happens when Ivy and Bennett plan their long-awaited getaway in *Seabreeze Honeymoon*.

Now that you've met April and her daughters May and June, visit them on nearby Crown Island in *Beach View Lane*, and discover this family's intriguing, feel-good story.

If you've read the Coral Cottage at Summer Beach series, join Marina and Kai and the rest of the Delavie-Moore family in a beach wedding to remember in *Coral Weddings*.

Keep up with my new releases on my website at JanMoran.com. Please join my VIP Reader's Club there to receive news about special deals and other goodies. Plus, find more fun and join other like-minded readers in my Facebook Reader's Group.

More to Enjoy

If this is your first book in the Seabreeze Inn at Summer Beach series, I invite you to revisit Ivy and Shelly as they renovate a historic beach house in *Seabreeze Inn*, the first book in the original Summer Beach series. In the Coral Cottage series, you'll meet Ivy's friend Marina in *Coral Cottage*.

If you'd like more sunshine and international travel, meet a group of friends in the *Love California* series, beginning with *Flawless* and an exciting trip to Paris.

Finally, I invite you to read my standalone family sagas, including *Hepburn's Necklace* and *The Chocolatier*, 1950s novels set in gorgeous Italy.

Most of my books are available in ebook, paperback or hardcover, audiobooks, and large print. And as always, I wish you happy reading!

More News

When I first wrote *Seabreeze Inn*, I thought the story would be a trilogy *with Seabreeze Summer* and *Seabreeze Sunset*. However, the response from readers was so great that I wrote a holiday special, *Seabreeze Christmas*. After that, *Seabreeze Weddings* flowed naturally.

And so on…until here we are.

By now, Ivy Bay and her family have become more than characters in a story. They're a part of my active imagination, and they seem to have taken on lives of their own in Summer Beach, along with the Moore and Delavie family in *Coral Cottage*.

While reviewing the final copy of this manuscript, I was on holiday in Peru to explore the Amazon and Machu Picchu. However, due to turmoil, a shelter-in-place order had been issued for the beautiful city of Cusco high in the Andes mountains. For the better half a week, our small tour group came together as a traveling family with our local guide (*muchas gracias* to Jimmy Ochoa!). As we supported and cared for each other, it reminded me of the true meaning of family, whether we're related or not. We're still joined by friendship, respect, concerns, goals, and laughter.

Thank you for reading and supporting the fun-loving, less-than-perfect Bay and Reina families (and their Summer Beach family of friends). They still manage to love each other and meet their challenges, just as we do.

Rest assured, there's more to come in Summer Beach. And on Crown Island, too. The inspiration for this new series that begins with *Beach View Lane* is Coronado Island, California, which has special meaning for me. The small beach community is just off the coast of Southern California and home to the historic Hotel del Coronado, one of my favorite beachside resorts.

Please visit my website and join my mailing list for all the latest excitement. I love dreaming up new surprises for you!

RECIPE: BUNDT PAN POUND CAKE

For as long as I can remember, my mother or grandmother would prepare this dense, fancy-looking bundt cake, which is easy to prepare from pantry staples. The name is derived from the ingredients: one pound each of butter, sugar, and flour. My mother would serve it to guests plain, or with a variety of light glazes for flavor. I thought I'd share this recipe in the story because it is such a fond family memory.

When I was a young girl, my grandmother taught me how to make this deceptively simple, delicious cake that we called Aunt Imogen's bundt cake. Imogen was my grandmother's sister-in-law, so this recipe has been in my family since at least 1952, when my grandmother sent the recipe to my mother, and probably longer.

The glaze is entirely optional, and we usually enjoyed the cake from the oven. My mother also used this recipe as a base for a chocolate marble cake by dividing the final mixture and adding

These days, I often use less sugar than called for in many recipes, so I've found that less sugar is just as tasty in this cake, too. Adjust to your taste.

Ingredients:

2 sticks butter, softened
2 cups sugar or (scant, 1 ½ cups)
5 eggs
2 cups sifted flour
1/2 tsp. salt
1/2 tsp. baking powder
1 tsp. vanilla
1 tsp. almond extract if desired

Instructions:

Pound Cake
1. Preheat the oven to 350 F.
2. To prevent sticking, prepare a bundt pan by greasing the interior with softened butter or cooking oil and dust with flour. Shake out excess flour. May also use a flour baking spray as a substitute.
3. In a large bowl, blend softened butter and sugar using a mixer.
4. Add eggs, one at a time and mix well.
5. Add baking powder and salt to flour and sift. Mix into wet ingredients a little at a time.
6. Pour into the prepared bundt pan.
7. Bake for one hour. Let cool before removing from pan.

Optional Lemon Glaze

1. In a medium bowl, combine lemon juice and confectioners' sugar.
2. Beat in the melted butter and 1 tablespoon water.
3. Poke small holes in the top of the cake with a toothpick or fork, and pour glaze over the top.

Optional Chocolate Marble

1. Divide cake mixture into two bowls.
2. Melt 4 to 6 ounces of bittersweet chocolate and add chocolate to one mixture.
3. Pour a little of the original mixture into the bundt pan, then
add a little of the chocolate mixture.
4. Alternate layers, ending with the original mixture on top.

ABOUT THE AUTHOR

JAN MORAN is a *USA Today* and a *Wall Street Journal* bestselling author of romantic women's fiction. A few of her favorite things include a fine cup of coffee, dark chocolate, fresh flowers, laughter, and music that touches her soul. She loves to travel, and her favorite places for inspiration are those rich with history and mystery and set against snowy mountains, palm-treed beaches, or sparkly city lights. Jan is originally from Austin, Texas, and a trace of a drawl still survives, although she has lived in Southern California near the beach for years.

Most of her books are available as audiobooks, and her historical fiction is translated into German, Italian, Polish, Dutch, Turkish, Russian, Bulgarian, Portuguese, and Lithuanian, and other languages.

If you enjoyed this book, please consider leaving a brief review online for your fellow readers where you purchased this book or on Goodreads or Bookbub.

To read Jan's other historical and contemporary novels, visit JanMoran.com. Join her VIP Readers Club mailing list and Facebook Readers Group to learn of new releases, sales and contests.